"You ha

The furrow by a flash of amusement.

"Yes. No. Oh, I don't know."

Nathan brushed a finger lightly down the bridge of her nose.

"Don't do that," she said, telling herself she didn't like his touches and private glances, but she knew better.

"Why?"

"Because."

He leaned closer. "That wasn't a good enough answer."

Steph arched away from him, worried about her reaction to his nearness. "Have you never heard of a little thing called personal space?"

He nodded and stepped toward her.

Steph fought the desire to step forward, to let him encircle her in his arms and smother her with kisses. What was she thinking? She moved away from him, again, like they were in some sort of dance. How could she escape, knowing her heart had turned against her head?

BEV HUSTON is an award-winning novelist whose first release, *Mix and Match,* was voted Favorite Novella of the Year by the members of ACRW. She lives in Maple Ridge, British Columbia, with her family who love being a part of her writing ministry. In addition to fiction, Bev also writes a Q&A computer column for *The Christian Communicator* and until 2003, she was the Senior Inspirational Reviewer for *Romantic Times.* She firmly believes that laughter is the best medicine and hopes each book brings a smile to the faces of her readers.

Let My Heart Go

Bev Huston

Heartsong Presents

To my son, J.D., who always comes up with a solution to my plotting problems; my daughter, Rebekah, whose encouragement knows no bounds; my husband, Sandy, who proofreads everything and is my number one fan—whether I deserve it or not.

Special thanks to my awesome critique partners, Jill and Sharon.

A note from the Author:
I love to hear from my readers! You may correspond with me by writing:

Bev Huston
Author Relations
PO Box 719
Uhrichsville, OH 44683

ISBN 1-59310-119-8

LET MY HEART GO

Our mission is to publish and distribute inspirational products offering exceptional value and biblical encouragement to the masses.

Scripture taken from the Holy Bible, New International Version®. NIV®. Copyright © 1973, 1978, 1984 by International Bible Society. Used by permission of Zondervan Publishing House. All rights reserved.

All of the characters and events in this book are fictitious. Any resemblance to actual persons, living or dead, or to actual events is purely coincidental.

PRINTED IN THE U.S.A.

one

Stephanie Harris slid into the hardback chair and checked her watch. She wasn't late. But that didn't stop Mr. Moses from casting a glance her way as he continued to speak. She tilted her chin and fixed an intent gaze on him, then crossed her arms.

If she didn't care so much for the troubled kids she worked with in the probation office she wouldn't be in this uncomfortable position. That, and the fact she couldn't say no to her boss. After checking out the eight men in the small, uncluttered classroom, she forced herself to concentrate.

"The most important thing to remember at the camp is that I'm always right," Mr. Moses said as he casually sat on the edge of a desk, swinging his legs.

What an ego. Just what she'd expect from this blond-haired, bronzed Tarzan type. Of course, she had to concede he looked better than the hunks who had portrayed the jungle man on the silver screen. No amount of clothing could hide his broad shoulders and well-defined arm muscles.

"I say that because, until I speak, you are in charge." Mr. Moses stood and moved closer to her. "Each of you will spend the day as a leader, cook, support person, whatever. If I have to intervene, it's because you're in danger. Is that clear?"

Everyone nodded. Everyone, that is, except Stephanie. Okay, maybe he wasn't all ego, but how could her clients gain anything from such an unstructured program? She couldn't risk a critical situation because some tanned survival guide had a strange way of viewing life.

"We'll need to travel about twenty-five miles every two days with heavy packs, but you guys shouldn't find it too strenuous."

Steph figured she'd heard enough but could not bring herself

5

to leave. Leaning against the chair back, arms still folded across her chest, she studied him.

He spoke with passion, his body language in sync with his words. Mr. Moses exuded a magnetic enthusiasm, and she had to shake her head to snap out of his force field.

"You'll find a list of what to wear and what to bring in your welcome envelope. If any of you didn't get one at the first class, see me later." He paused. "And, guys, don't buy cheap boots. You'll need thick-soled ones since the ground can get as hot as 180 degrees."

One hundred and eighty degrees? Phew. His words alone made her feel hot. Without thinking, she picked up a nearby piece of paper and fanned herself. Moments later, she stopped, feeling more than a little foolish. Mr. Moses' voice reclaimed her attention.

"Are you all right, Miss?" He stepped even closer, flashing an irresistible smile.

Stephanie sank farther into her seat and nodded. She felt as though she had drifted back ten years to her high school days. This time, though, the teacher was interesting, not to mention good-looking.

"Don't disturb the animal life out there," he said, as if he'd never been interrupted. "We'll camp about two hundred yards from each oasis so we don't hinder their drinking. You'll want to pay close attention to where you walk or put your hands, because snakes. . ."

The instructor's voice faded into the background again as Stephanie let her mind wander to consider all the reasons this could be a bad idea. Snakes would be at the top of the list, without a doubt.

Mr. Moses cleared his throat. "One other thing. We don't need any super-egos or daredevils out there. If no one has any questions, that's it for today, guys. See you back here on Monday. Tuesday we hit the trail."

"I've got a question," one of the men said. "How heavy are our packs?"

"Close to forty pounds."

Forty pounds! Reason number two, Stephanie decided. None of her kids could be expected to carry such a heavy load for ten days in the scorching desert heat.

"Anything else?" He looked around the room. "No? Okay. Spend the weekend relaxing, and pray for good weather next week!"

The group disbanded and the room soon emptied. She held her breath as the instructor approached and introduced himself.

"Nathaniel Moses," he said, offering his hand. "You must be Stephanie Harris." His grip felt strong, though the handshake lasted only a moment. Blue eyes twinkled as he held her gaze.

"Nice to meet you."

"So, I hear we're going to do a test camp for some of your clients. What is it you call them, first-timers?"

"That's yet to be decided," she replied, watching his smile falter. This was not the first time Steph's boss, Phil, had talked her into considering unconventional methods in her work. However, this had to be the worst idea yet. Assisting troubled kids back into mainstream society had been her dream. But lack of funding and heavy caseloads dampened any rewards, and her first-time offenders often became repeat offenders. A troubling fact for both Steph and her clients. Still, she did everything within her power to help.

"Yet to be decided?" He sounded confused.

"I'm only here to observe and then advise my boss."

"I see." He reached for a Burning Bush Adventures brochure from his heavy wooden desk. "So what can I do to help the decision along? We're very accommodating, you know. We can part the Red Sea, cast mountains into the ocean. You name it." He laughed at his own joke and held out the pamphlet to her.

"A little sure of yourself, aren't you?" Stephanie said. Compunction caused her to take the offered material. Personally, she had nothing against this man, but she couldn't retract her claws, like a lioness protecting her cubs. With arrogance like his, he could be dangerous—and perhaps not just for her clients.

"That's the purpose of this camp," he stated matter-of-factly.

"To turn everyone into you?"

"Hang on." He held up his hands then sat down on the desk. "I think you've got the wrong idea. I'm here to help. This camp has worked in numerous states. It's a proven method."

"Is it a proven method with city kids who've never stepped foot in a desert?" Steph didn't give him an opportunity to answer. "I don't think so. Studies show this type of boot camp is not as effective as you claim. My job is to help my clients get back on track and stay out of trouble. Pushing them to exhaustion carrying heavy packs in the heat doesn't seem to be the way to go." Her tone softened as she looked into his eyes and sensed she'd wounded him. "I don't want to tangle with you, Mr. Moses. My clients need to be protected and have someone care about them. No one else seems to."

"With all due respect, Miss Harris, I believe in my methods. We're too soft on our kids these days. We're afraid of them. We don't say no to them—"

Stephanie stepped back and refused to make further eye contact. "Perhaps that's how you handle your children, Mr. Moses, but it's not the way my clients have been treated. They've been forced to toe the line or take a beating. Or they've been neglected and sought attention by acting out or getting into trouble. These kids require some compassion and understanding to help them over the rough spots. Forcing them into unknown territory will damage them further."

"Then we're at an impasse," he said with a sigh. "If you feel that way about my course, I really don't want you or your kids."

She detected a note of sadness in his voice and, oddly, it tugged at her. "I'm glad you feel that way." She reached for her purse and placed it firmly over her shoulder. "It's nothing personal."

He reached out to shake her hand once again. "If I can ever be of service, don't hesitate to call."

She felt like dirt. She'd been needlessly harsh when Phil was the one she wanted to strangle. "Thank you for your time," she replied, noticing he still held her hand. She pulled it back from his grasp.

"You're welcome," he said as he walked her toward the door.

Suddenly her stomach reminded her that she hadn't had lunch. She quickened her pace and hoped he hadn't heard her body's complaint. The awkward moment became worse as she realized he had stirred some unusual feelings in her. *He's definitely not my type.*

Stephanie didn't look back as she crossed the parking lot to her car. She gave the door a good yank and was relieved when it opened without a problem. After slipping into her seat, she grabbed her sunglasses from the dashboard and put them on.

A few embarrassing moments passed before the engine turned over and she could leave Mr. Moses' parking lot, and his sight. She pulled a tissue from her purse and patted the perspiration trickling down the back of her neck. Could it be all that talk about the desert heat that caused her reaction, or something more? More as in Mr. Moses? She didn't want to think about that right now.

A few blocks away, Stephanie parked and entered the only diner in the area. She slid into a booth and eyed the menu. The waitress brought a cup of coffee, took her order, then left.

Lowering her face into her hands, Stephanie closed her eyes and massaged a nagging throb at her temples. She sighed. *Maybe I'm being too harsh on Mr. Moses.* She glanced up to find him striding, with his signature air of confidence, into the diner. *Or maybe not. Is he stalking me now?* She busied herself with the sugar to keep from watching him step toward her.

"Heard your stomach rumbling so I figured you'd stop here," he said as she looked up at him. He gave her a lopsided grin. "I saw your car and—" He hesitated. "Look, I think we started off on the wrong foot. Mind if I join you?"

Her heartbeat quickened, but her mind slowed. "Well, umm—"

"Great." He seated himself across from her.

Steph frowned. The waitress appeared with another cup of coffee, and he ordered lunch.

Of all the nerve.

"Miss Harris, I must apologize for upsetting you. I'm afraid you have the wrong idea about me."

"On the contrary. I understand your type perfectly. I realize if you didn't display a very strong, confident image, you wouldn't have a business. However, I have to worry about the influence you could have over my clients. I feel it's unhealthy."

"I beg your pardon?"

"You heard me, Mr. Moses." She picked up her coffee cup.

"Call me Nathan. May I call you—?"

"Miss Harris," she said, putting the mug back down.

A hint of a smile appeared at the corners of his mouth. He took a long sip of his hot drink, then said, "Miss Harris, I'm not a psychiatrist—"

"Neither am I."

"Psychologist, then."

She shook her head, but he continued. "I know people. I've been around them all my life and studied them, wanting to know what makes them tick. As a result, I've come to appreciate God's handiwork in creating us." He paused. "I grew up without the benefit of parents, and what I've become is due to the independence I gained making it on my own."

"I think a certain Mr. Anthony Moses is the reason you're doing so well." She raised her cup again and took a sip this time, hoping to hide the pleasure she felt in catching him off guard.

"You've done your homework."

"I have."

"Then you know about my life before he took me in?"

Did I miss something on his website? "Not everything. I know you didn't start this business without help—even though that's what you seem to be implying."

"I wasn't implying anything. I'd taken refuge in Anthony's car when he found me. He'd been lonely since his wife had died. I understood that." Nathan seemed to search her face for a reaction, but she remained stoic. "My only memories were of the group home I'd run away from. So we were good for each other. I took his last name, which I think made him proud. He left me some money in his will when he passed away."

The tenderness in his voice as he spoke about the senior

Mr. Moses touched Stephanie, but she resolved to keep this strictly business. "It's a moving story, Mr.—"

"Nathan."

"Nathan. But it won't work with my kids. Even if you've done a lot of good for other people. I can't, in all honesty, agree with you."

"I don't get it," he said without accusation. "What makes you so certain it won't work?"

"Aside from the results of a study at the University of Maryland that proves it won't, I think it's cruel and unusual punishment."

He laughed heartily. "And I suppose you want to take them on one of those yoga and meditation bus tours instead. Teach them to get in touch with their true feelings by humming."

"It's quite obvious that we have very different perspectives on life." Her words came out with clipped deliberation.

"That would appear to be the first thing we've both agreed on." He picked up his cup and stood. "Good day, Miss Harris."

Stephanie watched as Nathaniel walked away. She didn't know whether to be angry or relieved. Lowering her head again, she peered from beneath her bangs while he found another seat.

She gritted her teeth and tried to calm herself. Had she approved this camp, Nathaniel Moses would have been a constant thorn in her side. He didn't believe in structure or rules—except one. He was always right. Her experience told her he might be hiding behind his own poor self-esteem. And yet, after all her mental berating of him, she found herself smiling. Plus, he *was* cute, in a Herculean sort of way, but she needed to get her mind off him. Now.

She pulled out her day planner and began scribbling notes. When the waitress brought her clubhouse sandwich, she couldn't finish it fast enough. She paid the check and left the diner—and Mr. Moses, once again.

❧

Twenty minutes later, Stephanie arrived back at work. She marched into her office, slamming the door behind her. The glass panels rattled. She'd barely taken a seat behind her desk when Phil knocked.

She looked up and saw that he'd opened the door a little and was waving a white handkerchief. Stephanie laughed. "Yes, Phil. You can come in."

"Bad day?" He dropped his football player frame onto the leather sofa across the room.

"You might say that."

"Gonna tell me about it?" He stretched out on the couch, folding his hands across his chest like a patient ready for psychoanalysis.

"Don't you want to wait for my report?" She shuffled some papers on her desk, eyeing him with caution.

"Do I?" He raised his eyebrows.

She smiled. She liked Phil a great deal. She appreciated his open rapport with the staff and his willingness to see things their way. He was a corrections officer turned administrator and knew his limitations. Sometimes.

She placed her hands palm-side down on her desk and began. "For starters, Mr. Nathaniel Moses is an egotistical know-it-all. In fact, I'm sure when he looks in the mirror he thinks he sees his better half! He has no structure. No guidelines. No real rules or goals for that so-called survival camp. Phil, do you know what he plans to do?" She stood and started to pace, struggling to control the rising pitch in her voice.

"He plans to have those kids walk twelve and a half miles every day carrying heavy packs. They have to withstand the grueling heat and, oh yes, he's always right." Stephanie regretted her outburst the instant she finished. But she could not have stopped herself any more than she could halt a speeding locomotive with her hands.

Phil raised his handkerchief with a grin. "I take it you two didn't see eye to eye."

"Eye to eye? We didn't even see toe-to-toe!" She dropped back into her chair.

Phil appeared startled. "I've never seen you like this. What's the real problem? You know not everyone is as, ah, organized as you." He swung his feet down and sat up.

Stephanie opened her mouth, but no words came out. *What is the real problem?* She took a deep breath and kicked off her shoes. As she distractedly rubbed her aching foot she thought for a moment. "The real problem is exactly what I said."

Phil shook his head. "There's more to it. You don't act like a hysterical female, ever. Why today?"

"I'm insulted."

"You've been insulted before, and it's never bothered you like this. What did the guy say?"

"No, you've insulted me."

"I have? When? Why didn't you tell me earlier?" Phil's eyebrows arched.

Stephanie closed her eyes and counted to ten fast. Opening her eyes, she said, "Not earlier. Now. When you called me hysterical."

"I thought you meant Mr. Moses insulted you."

She sighed. "I'll write out a report."

"When can I expect it?"

She felt him watching her as she picked up a file. "When do you want it?"

He leaned forward and rested his forearms on his thighs, hands clasped. "After you've taken the course."

"That's funny."

"It's not meant to be. How soon can you do it?"

Steph sucked in a breath. "What's going on here? First you ask me to check this place out. *Which* I did. And in my professional opinion, *which* up until a few moments ago counted for something, I believe this is not a practical venue. Now I offer to send you a detailed report, *which* you decline until I've gone and survived ten days in a hot, dusty desert."

"Relax," Phil said. "I don't understand what's got you so wound up. We agreed you'd take the course. You can even choose your other 'survivor' members. So what's the problem?"

Another longsuffering sigh escaped. Stephanie had worked with Phil long enough to know he wouldn't push without good reason. She'd have to look at it from another angle.

Perhaps she could persuade Mr. Moses to tailor the course for her clients. Or reduce the walking distance and weight of the packs. Surely he could step down from his pedestal long enough to revamp his camp a tiny bit. Then she would see firsthand how the kids reacted without too much hardship and still have all the ammo she needed for Phil.

"I'll go through the files and try to locate some possible participants," she conceded. "You realize you'll be without me for ten days. I don't know how you'll handle it."

He pulled his truce-hanky from his pocket once again and placed it dramatically across his forehead. "We'll manage somehow."

"And, Phil, don't expect me to hold everything together out there in the middle of nowhere, then come back here and fix whatever goes wrong while I'm gone." She felt herself smile despite the situation.

"Deal," was his only reply as he got up and left.

≈

"What do you think?"

Nathan shuffled the papers, laid them flat on his desk, and turned to look up at Stephanie Harris. Her apple-green eyes sparkled, and a small smile tipped the corners of her pink lips. "I can't."

She tossed her blonde hair back over her shoulder. "You can't? Or you won't?"

Nathan had felt remorseful all weekend because of their first encounter on Friday. In fact, while in church Sunday, he prayed he'd be more civil to Miss Harris if he ever had the displeasure of meeting her again. *Who would have thought it would be this soon?*

For such a petite, soft-featured woman, she sure could be feisty. He couldn't escape her determined gaze—a gaze that led him to believe her prickly attitude hid a wealth of pain. And somehow he felt his answer to her question would inflict even more hurt. "Honestly? Both."

"I see." She stood and turned to leave.

"I don't think you do." He took her arm, intending to guide

her back. At first, he could feel her yield, then she wrenched free of his grasp.

He saw fire in her eyes. "You don't need to remind me that you are always right, like some omnipotent almighty. Your students might buy it, but I don't."

Ouch. "Where did you ever get an idea like that?"

"You said so yourself. You told those guys right here in this room."

"Okay, truce," he said in a calm tone. "First off, there is only one God and it ain't me. Second, I apologize if we have misunderstood each other. I don't know how things keep getting twisted, but I'd sure like to sort them out."

She opened her mouth and then shut it without saying a word.

He wanted to laugh. It was the first time he'd seen her speechless. And even though he should be mad as a disturbed rattler, he understood. He could even understand her concerns—to a degree, of course. What he didn't understand was all the energy she put into being angry. *What did Anthony always say? Anger's just an emotion away from smoldering passion.* Hmm, if his old mentor had been right, then he would have to be careful.Nathan resisted a laugh. It would explain why he had always been angry with Jill Slater as a kid. Everything she did had made him crazy. Funny he should think of that now while talking with Miss Harris.

"I said, can we discuss this?" She sounded impatient as she paced in front of his desk.

Nathan caught the tail end of her question and hastily replied to cover his inattention, "Sure. Over dinner?" Somehow he'd have to convince her he couldn't make the changes to the camp she desired. Reducing the load for the females would cause problems. He knew from experience that women wanted to be treated as equals—and in his eyes they were. If he could get Miss Harris to relax in a more casual setting, she'd hear him out.

"We've already tried one meal together," she said, her stiff shoulders now relaxed in surrender.

Is that a smile she's giving me? "Anthony always said if at first you don't succeed—"

"Give up." She laughed.

Nathan felt captivated as his gaze met hers, and he worried he had a silly grin plastered from ear to ear. "Miss Harris—"

"Call me Stephanie."

"I'd like that, and dinner," he replied, hoping it wasn't the calm before the storm.

Together they walked to the door. As Stephanie left, she agreed to meet him later that evening. He watched her for a moment then returned to his desk, certain he would be unable to accomplish a thing for the rest of the day.

"Lord, help me," he prayed aloud. "You know how important this state contract is to me. To my business. You know what will happen if I don't get it. What about my promise?" Nathan unclenched his fists. "Help me get through to Stephanie. Please."

Though they had only just met, she had already gotten under his skin. Could he be honest and still win this contract? Would it be worth what he would have to go through? He suspected a bite from a Gila monster would be preferable to a survival camp with Stephanie, regardless of his financial needs.

Nathan gave an exclamation of disgust with himself. *Please give me patience, Lord—and a thick skin at dinner this evening.*

⁂

Damian Farrow resisted the urge to frown as he entered the Burning Bush Adventures trailer. He eyed the old school type desks and life-size adventure posters on the wall. *This guy must be a typical jock.* "I'm looking for Nathanial Moses," he said while loosening his tie.

"You found him." A rugged-looking man rose and extended his hand. "You must be Mr. Farrow."

"Damian."

Moses motioned for him to take a seat then sat back down at his desk. "It's a pleasure to meet you. Your father has done a lot of good for the state of Utah, as well as here at home, of course."

"Thanks," Damian replied, reminding himself to play nice.

It irked him that everyone mentioned his father. What about the good he'd done for this sorry small town? Seventy thousand people had him to thank for the new sports complex, but did they? No. They just assumed it was his father again. If they put Alex Farrow's pedestal any higher he'd get a nosebleed.

"I hear you've got a hand in the planning of the mega mall on the outskirts of town."

Damian struggled to keep his voice calm. "That's one of my father's latest projects." *Which I hope to stop.* He put down his briefcase and cut to the point. "So, Moses, like I said the other day, I've heard some impressive things about your company. That's why I set up this meeting."

"Why don't you take off your jacket while I get us some water?"

Damian nodded but didn't move. He felt safe in his power suits. "As you know, I've got a lot of irons in the fire here. I know who's thriving and who's barely surviving." Damian didn't miss the fact that Nathan swallowed hard at his comment. He knew business had slacked off, thanks to innuendoes he'd been spreading around town. Moses needed Damian and his money right about now, and it would only be a matter of minutes before he jumped at the offer.

"I suppose you do." Nathan handed the water to Damian.

"I own a number of establishments, too. That doesn't mean I don't want what's best for the community. I have more than I'll ever need so I can afford to be generous."

"I must admit, you have me wondering why you're interested in my company." Nathan lowered himself back into his seat.

"Burning Bush has a lot of potential. The hits to your website are phenomenal for such a small outfit. With the right backing, you could turn this into our number-one tourist trade. And I'm all for bringing in visitors. The economical benefits are worth it alone."

"I don't think this is the type of business that could support such ideals."

"Why not let me be the judge of that? Contrary to popular belief, I wasn't born in this suit," he said with a chuckle.

Nathan smiled and handed him a brochure. "Well, this is what we do."

Damian's stomach dropped to his feet as he skimmed the text and stared at the pictures. How far would he go with this charade? He didn't have to wonder long. He knew he would do whatever it took to usurp his father.

"If you'll pardon my saying this, Mr. Farrow, I'm not quite sure I understand what sort of involvement you desire with Burning Bush Adventures."

"Like I said, I know who's doing well and who isn't. I think you've got potential, but despite the web hit numbers, business is slow, right?"

Nathan swallowed again. "So what do you have in mind?"

"That's what I'm here to discuss." Damian's smile faded as he studied Nathan's emotionless expression.

"Of course, that's after you check everything out thoroughly, right?"

So the guy has brains. Too bad. "Right."

"I've got a full load leaving tomorrow morning, first thing. There's always room for one more. Why don't you join us?"

Sweat beaded on Damian's forehead. "That's too soon. I need to make arrangements. What about the next one?" He tucked Nathan's brochure into his briefcase and snapped it shut. His stomach clenched as his gaze fixed on the poster of a man dangling from a mountain perched high in the sky.

"We've got a test camp coming up with some youth on probation," Nathan said, sounding reluctant. "Don't know if that would interest you."

"Sure. I've got another quick appointment this afternoon. Why don't we meet at El Español Mira this evening so I can learn more about your excursions?"

"I've already got a business meeting there this evening. Let me just give you a few quick details before you go," he offered.

Nathan briefed Damian on his schedule and advised him about the test camp. Things looked very promising once Damian learned about the teens and their caseworker. This camp would be a piece of cake—and another rung on his ladder to success.

෨

Nathan felt restless as he tidied his office after Damian left. Could this mean he wouldn't have to depend on Stephanie and a state contract? If so, maybe he didn't need to see her for dinner tonight, either. Oddly, that thought triggered a sense of disappointment.

Since Stephanie presented so much opposition and Damian could be an answer to prayer, maybe he could relax. If Damian provided some sort of financial backing or major promotion, there would be no need for Miss Harris. Or was he jumping ahead of God?

Nathan decided he'd better be prepared. He would have several stories to share with Stephanie that would put her mind at ease and prove that women didn't want to be treated as any less able than men. She would soon see her fears were ungrounded.

In reality, though, he knew nothing he could do would ease her mind if she didn't want it eased. She'd probably insist he move the water sources closer, or something just as impossible. What was her problem? *Lots of women have taken harsher courses than this.* He stared at a desk photo from an Alpine course in the Sierra Nevadas.

He chuckled. Almost everyone in that group had been young, except for this one slightly overweight woman named Tilly. Even mothering five children hadn't prepared her for the grueling twenty-three-day course. He'd had no doubt Tilly would make it to the end, but she hadn't felt that way. There were times when he was certain she had reached her breaking point, but Tilly had not only survived, she'd been a new person when they returned. Face peeling from the wind and sun, hands raw from the climb, blisters on her feet—yet at the end Tilly declared she wouldn't trade the experience for anything.

Hmm, maybe Stephanie did have cause for concern.

He anticipated the evening with Stephanie like a summer thunderstorm in the desert. Lovely to enjoy—if you were watching from a safe distance.

two

Steph stared at Nathan's business card as she waited for him at the El Español Mira. *What am I doing here?* A surge of skepticism welled up inside her, but her usual level-headedness prevailed. The purpose of their meeting was simply to discuss what could be done to make this trip more palatable.

In the back of her mind she checked off which clients would be best suited for such an excursion. So far, only one seemed capable. Coming up with another five would be difficult.

She took a sip from her ice water and looked around the restaurant. She could feel her face flush when he arrived at that exact moment.

"Been here long?" He smiled as he lowered himself into the comfortable chair.

"A few minutes." She felt an odd whirl in her stomach. The man seated before her couldn't possibly be the same person she'd met earlier. He wore a crisp white dress shirt and a double-breasted suit that enhanced his muscular physique. His aftershave was subtle and inviting, like his luminescent blue eyes.

"Sorry, I had a visitor and the meeting went longer than planned."

Could it have been a woman? Steph cringed inwardly at her runaway thoughts. "No problem." She needed air. She picked up the menu and buried her face in it.

Nathan followed suit. "I hear the rattlesnake is quite good."

"Yes, I've heard that, too. But I think I'll stick to the mesquite chicken." She closed the menu and placed it beside her plate then studied him while he continued to read.

He glanced up at her, and she diverted her eyes. *Come on, Steph, you know how the game is played. You've got a job to do. You know better than to melt. That's what Mr. Moses wants.* "So let's get right to the point, shall we?"

"I thought we could eat first. Let our meal digest and then. . ."

"And then what?" There was that caustic tone in her voice again. She bit her bottom lip.

"You don't trust anyone, do you?" His words weren't accusing, and she even sensed merriment in his voice.

"And you find that funny?" *Cool it. He's probably just trying to get through the meal, so leave the analyzing for later.*

"Tell me a little about yourself." He sounded sincere.

She paused for a moment as she gathered her thoughts. "I've only been at my job for a few years, but it is the one thing in life that gives me pleasure."

"That's good, since we spend three quarters of our waking lives working."

She took a sip of water. "I pride myself on being able to care for these troubled kids, yet I can keep a level head, thus enabling me to assist them effectively." She lowered her glass. "Until the case is closed," she added, her voice laden with heaviness.

His eyes clouded. "Don't the kids recognize your emotional distance?"

"I—" She stopped, forcing herself to repress her rising anger.

"I didn't mean that the way it sounded. We all have different ways of protecting ourselves. You probably know that better than I do. Kids respond well when some form of emotional bond is created. I can tell the kids at the camp that I want them to survive, but until I face the same hardships and work hand-in-hand with them, I'm just another adult pushing their buttons."

Steph shifted in her chair. "That may be the case with you, but my clients recognize that I have to work within certain boundaries to assist them. I have rules I must follow, but I do my best to—"

"You can still follow the rules," he interjected calmly. "But have you ever opened up and given a part of yourself to them?"

"What good would that do?"

"I don't know. Help them to see you're human? You were a teenager once. Didn't you ever do anything wrong growing up?"

She choked back a feeling of panic. He couldn't know about something she regretted to this day.

"I'm interrupting you. Please forgive me." Nathan took a long drink of water, but she could tell his eyes were still on her. Watching.

Stephanie jumped at the chance to move on. "I've got a pretty full caseload, but I like the demanding pace."

Nathan leaned forward and asked, "And in your spare time, what do you do?"

"Spare time? What's that? I usually work on my cases over the weekend."

"Doesn't your boyfriend mind?"

Her face grew hot. "There's no one significant in my life."

"What about family? Brothers and sisters?"

She steeled herself to answer without emotion. "I have no family."

"I'm sorry. Guess we have something in common."

The waiter arrived to take their order. Stephanie appreciated the interlude. When she had finished ordering, she watched Nathan as he spoke. It didn't surprise her that he ordered a non-caffeinated soft drink. She knew his type. The thrill of the outdoors, the challenge of the impossible were what gave this man his highs. *He's certainly a classic case. Not everyone likes the great outdoors—in fact, what's so great about it?*

"What about your past, Mr. Moses?"

"Nathan," he reminded her with a wink. "I think we discussed it earlier."

"Yes, that's right. Orphaned at a young age and then rescued by Anthony Moses."

"I think rescued is a very appropriate word. I was a lonely, bitter kid. Angry at the world for all its injustice. I didn't think it fair that all the other kids had parents and I didn't."

"That's normal." *I sound so clinical.* She played with her napkin.

"But Mr. Moses seemed to understand. He helped me a great deal."

"Can I assume because you still call him Mr. Moses that he maintained some level of emotional distance, yet managed to be of great assistance to you?" *Don't smile. Keep a straight face. You've got him.*

"Nice try." He seemed to say it with such delight. She watched as a smile spread across his tanned face. "Anthony Moses and I shared a common bond. Grief. I was only a kid at the time and didn't feel comfortable calling him Dad or anything like that. And he called me Mr. Christian."

Steph raised an eyebrow and waited for an explanation.

"It was a joke we shared."

"But why Mr. Christian?" She could listen to him talk for hours—well, maybe not in the classroom, but here in the dimly lit restaurant. Soft music played in the background, and no one bothered them.

"My real name is Nathaniel Christian. I only took Moses as my last name right before he died. If not for his strong faith, I'm sure I never would have survived."

Stephanie felt a lump rise in her throat. *Guess my faith lacked strength*, she thought with bitterness. She forced the idea from her mind. She needed to change the course of the conversation. It would be safer for her if she kept focused, determined to protect her kids. "So you two sorted out your problems and here you are."

"Just like that?" He snapped his fingers. "Actually, not quite. But, yes, here I am."

Ready, willing, and able to help you, I bet you're thinking. Well, Mr. Moses, I don't need your help. She needed to keep drawing the line. They were here to discuss his camp and why she wasn't going to recommend it, yet somehow she kept getting sidetracked.

"I like to think I'm making a difference," he continued.

A pang of regret filled her. He seemed like such a nice guy. *Why does he get to me?* "Another thing we have in common," she offered, hoping to lessen her guilt.

In time, thanks to the right atmosphere, the conversation eased into a more relaxed flow. They talked about movies, songs, and current events. Though it appeared their opinions differed, in reality she wanted to keep her guard up. Trivia questions and mini-parables spilled forth with ease.

"What do you mean you can't name the top disaster films of the 1970s?"

Stephanie laughed. "I can't."

"Wanna hint?"

"Of course not, that'd be cheating."

"Oh, and you think the little trivia police will cuff you?"

"Okay, how about *Airport 1975*."

Nathaniel looked around the room and leaned forward. "Who helped you?" he asked in a mock threatening tone. "They're dead, you know. I don't like to lose."

Of course, she knew he was teasing, but something made her wonder if a hint of truth laced his comment. He obviously preferred adrenaline to calm. If she were honest, she had to admit he reminded her of someone she'd already lost—her father.

Why did she have to meet this man under these circumstances? She could overlook his ego—most of the time. She could even get in better shape for the occasional bike ride and maybe even learn to love camping. Stephanie knew she'd crossed the line with that last thought.

"I'm waiting."

She'd been so busy daydreaming, she wasn't sure what he was referring to. "I have no idea why."

"Ah, you're back." He laughed and reached over to pat the back of her hand.

She wanted to pull away, but that would make her discomfort obvious. "Here's one for you, Mr. Christian." She decided she liked calling him by his former name. It had a certain style. "What is the most often used letter in written English?"

"Dear John?"

She groaned.

"Oh, don't go getting intellectual on me. Next you'll be showing me some inkblots and asking what they mean."

"Okay, how about this one? Name the top film of 1956."

"Not fair, I wasn't even born then."

"And you think I was when you asked me that difficult Dickens question?"

Steph watched as Nathaniel pretended to be thinking hard, brow furrowed, bottom lip protruding. She leaned back, stifling a yawn as she glanced at her watch. The hour was late, and he needed to be up early. *I better move this along.* "Wanna clue?" she teased.

"Sure."

"In the short time I've known you, I think you've alluded to him at least a dozen times."

"Will there be anything else?" the waiter asked as he began to clear the table.

Nathaniel ordered two coffees and returned to the conversation. "In 1956, you say?"

She nodded.

"Right. Must have been *The Ten Commandments*."

"See, I told you it wasn't hard." She batted his forearm in a playful swipe as it rested on the table.

Everything seemed so right. That is, until Nathan began talking about his involvement in his church. A closed-door subject for her. She had waited while Nathan said grace when the meal had arrived, but that would be the extent of her indulgence in things concerning a Supreme Being.

"I'm not as involved in my church as I'd like to be, but my schedule is anything but routine." He sat back in the chair and appeared content from the meal.

"We used to go to church," she said in a sort of tiptoe voice, as if she should be ashamed to admit such a thing. *Get out while you can. It's been pleasant so far. Don't start another battle.* But she couldn't stop. A yearning for a time long ago compelled her to share some of her story. "My mother had a beautiful voice and sang in the choir. I'd give anything to hear her sing one more time." Regret sent an untouchable ache through her.

Nathan leaned forward and reached for her hand again. She fought the desire to pull back once more. "I'm so sorry."

"I'm over it." She tossed his empathy away, as if saying the words would make them true.

"You no longer go to church?"

"I don't have time," she said, but she knew in her heart this wasn't the truth.

"But you still have a relationship with God?" His tone sounded light, yet she felt defensive.

"I don't think it matters to anyone but me what my relationship with God is." *I should have just told him I don't believe anymore.*

He sat back and raised his hands in a show of surrender. "You're right. It's a personal thing."

She wished he'd touch her hand again. Maybe there could be something more to this man than she had first thought. She chastised herself for jumping to conclusions.

When the conversation turned to the camp, her chest felt tight. She wrung her hands beneath the table.

"I know you're worried, but I have an idea," he said. "I'm wondering if part of your fear is the short preparation time. Two classes are more than enough for the guys I'm taking out tomorrow, but I'll do as many classes as you want for your group. I'll even teach CPR and basic first aid. I figure two classes a week for eight weeks should be enough. You'll see that I cover everything before we even hit the dirt."

"Most of the people taking your camp do so of their own free will," Steph began, now twisting her water glass between her hands. "But these kids will want to be anywhere but there. Creating a very different scenario." Did that sound like pleading? She hoped not.

"I used to be one of those kids, remember?"

"I don't know." Her arguments were losing force, and she knew she needed to separate the man from the job. Hard to do when up to this point all she'd ever had was her career. But files didn't keep her warm at night or comfort her in moments of sadness and loss. Nathan's voice interrupted her thoughts.

"I know you're unsure based on your studies and research. But will you trust me, Stephanie?"

Hearing him say her name for the first time caused her stomach to flip-flop. She resisted her initial reaction and responded, "I'll trust you until something goes wrong. Then we do it my way." Her words came out stronger than she had intended, but more than likely it was because she really wanted to say, "Always. I'll trust you always."

"Nathan, good to see you," an impeccably dressed stranger practically shouted as he neared their table. He reached out and touched them both on the shoulder. Stephanie stiffened, and she could tell by the frown on Nathan's face that he had a similar reaction.

Nathan introduced Damian Farrow to Stephanie. She could see the resemblance to Alex Farrow, Damian's father, in his dark eyes, and he had the famous Farrow frown. She'd barely shaken his hand when he launched into a discourse.

"I'm looking forward to our next excursion," he said. "A group of delinquents and their caseworker. Bet that will cure what ails them."

Stephanie could tell by Nathan's wince that he didn't find the comments funny. "Yes, well," she started. "It just so happens I'm that caseworker."

Mr. Farrow didn't have the decency to blush or apologize, and she wondered if he'd been drinking something stronger than a cola. If so, she'd have to ensure Nathan enforced a no-alcohol rule.

"I'm only having a little fun, Moses. I believe in the camp. Honest. I know I'll come back a *richer* person, too."

Steph picked up on the way he said the word *richer*, but she decided to let Nathan handle him.

"Well, we do have strict rules—"

"Yeah, yeah, I know. Why not tell me more about this pretty little lady? Or is she off limits?" He winked and sounded pleased with himself.

She felt sorry for Nathan. Their gazes met, and although she expected him to be angry, he merely seemed compassionate.

Nathan tapped Mr. Farrow's arm and nodded toward the aisle. "If I'm not mistaken, that woman heading in our direction is looking for you. I think it would be best if you met her halfway."

Mr. Farrow paled and nodded, then turned and left.

A sense of relief flooded Steph, and she appreciated that Nathan did not discuss Damian Farrow further. An ill feeling about him permeated the air and caused a lingering discomfort for her.

After paying the bill, Nathan stood up and pulled out her chair. When he gazed into her eyes, she could feel a blush rising to her cheeks again. *This is ridiculous. I don't like the way this man lives his life. I don't like his silly old boot camp. And this is only the start of my long list of dislikes.*

Stepping out into the night air, Nathan casually draped his jacket over her shoulders. They wandered slowly to her car. Stephanie wished the night weren't over and knew that was not a good sign. Maybe the time had come to switch to Plan B. Whatever that was.

Nathan leaned closer and brushed his knuckles down her cheek. "Thanks for a fun night. See you in ten days."

She handed back his jacket and stood by her car as he sauntered over to his jeep. She suddenly realized her hand rested over the same cheek he had touched. Yes, she definitely needed a new game plan.

やa

The next morning, Stephanie could not keep her mind on her job. Her thoughts reverted to the prior evening with Nathan.

The dinner had been more than pleasant. And if she had had any doubt Nathan loved the desert, none lingered now. He'd described the desert and his experiences there with the excitement of a child. She could tell he never grew tired of his trips.

Yet Stephanie still couldn't understand what all the commotion was about. All she could visualize was a lot of dust and dry things. Still, she delighted in the way Nathan's face lit up whenever he spoke about the arid place. All of which caused her to struggle with her feelings and recognize how inconsistent she had become. He seemed to have a zest for life, despite the hand that had been dealt him. She both envied and resented that. Spending time with him caused her to realize her unhappiness. A reminder she didn't need.

"Got enough files pulled out there?" Phil asked as he

stepped into her office.

Stephanie sighed and nodded.

Phil leaned over and placed the back of his hand on her forehead. "Hmm, no fever."

"Meaning?"

"What? No quick-witted reply for my comment? Only a simple question? Something must be wrong. Are you ill?"

"Guess I'm too hot to care."

"Actually, it's not that bad in here." Phil picked up a folder, flipped through it, and then placed it back on the pile. "It sure beats the outer office area."

"It feels hot," she said, straightening the stack of folders and staring at him.

"Maybe you need a break." He flopped down on the sofa. "How's it coming, by the way?"

"I've got two so far. Finding four more is like panning for gold."

"You never disappoint me, Steph. I know you'll find them."

"I hope so. Only ten days before the first class, and I need to get a list of about eight in case someone backs out at the last minute."

Phil laughed as he stood to leave. "I've never known you not to get your way."

Well, if that were true, Buster, I wouldn't be going on this trip. "Are you saying I'm good at what I do or I'm spoiled?"

"Both."

He ducked when Steph tossed a paper clip at him. Good thing she liked Phil. "I see, so you're saying I'm spoiled good?"

"Not at all. First, that's grammatically incorrect; second, I don't care for that active listening stuff you're always spouting off."

"Latent learning," she mumbled, pretending to write it down. "So you do listen to me occasionally?"

"Nah, that's just my conditioned response." He laughed and moved toward the door.

"You amaze me, Phil. Next you'll be explaining the social clock to me."

"I will?"

"Sure. And after that, you can take my place in the desert." She smiled at him ever so sweetly.

"Never."

Stephanie breathed a sigh of relief when Phil left. She forced herself to concentrate on the stack of folders piled before her and buried her thoughts.

Shortly before noon, her secretary buzzed that someone wished to see her. As she stepped from her office, disappointment settled upon Stephanie when she recognized the man from the restaurant. What did she think? That it would be Nathan? How silly.

"Miss Harris, I need to see you. May I speak with you in your office?"

Damian Farrow appeared less obtrusive this morning, and she motioned for him to enter. She seated herself behind her desk and waved him toward a nearby chair.

"First, let me apologize for my inappropriate behavior last night. Second, as Nathan's partner, I want you to know if you need anything, you can call me."

She blinked in surprise.

Mr. Farrow rushed on, never breaking eye contact. "Since I'm taking the next camp, I want to ensure we have a good working relationship."

Steph raised an eyebrow. "I see. I assumed Mr. Moses would lead the excursion." Disappointment seized her.

Mr. Farrow's smile remained fixed. "Of course, he'll still lead. But I think it's important we trust one another out there."

I don't even trust you in my office. "And you're here to facilitate that?"

He stiffened. "Let's start with getting to know one another. Let me take you to lunch."

She gestured toward the files around her. "I've got a lot of work to do as you can see, Mr. Farrow. Thank you for your offer."

"Please call me Damian. And it could be a quick bite—painless, too." He laughed at his little joke.

"I'm sorry," she replied.

"If it's because of last night, let me assure you I don't normally act that way. I'd had some very bad news and was having difficulty dealing with it."

She nodded but remained silent. *Let's see if he'll hang himself with his smooth words.*

"Why don't I bring back something for you? A sandwich, perhaps?"

"I appreciate your offer, but I do have to finalize the group and work with our legal representative drafting the release forms."

"Oh, that's not necessary. Those forms are all prepared at Burning Bush Adventures."

"Yes, quite right, but they indemnify and release Burning Bush Adventures. Our clients will also be signing such a form in our favor, too."

"Perhaps I could drop by with copies of our paperwork for your lawyer to review."

He seemed too eager to please. "Not necessary. I appreciate the offer. Now if you'll excuse me."

"I'll be in touch then. Don't hesitate to call." He rose to leave.

"Perhaps I could have one of your cards," Stephanie asked, almost as an afterthought.

His eyes darkened. Did she detect a flash of anger? "I don't believe I have any with me at the moment. I'll drop one off later."

She viewed this as a ploy to enable him to return, and she didn't like it. In a formal, authoritative voice she dismissed him knowing he would not appreciate being treated that way. Everyone in town revered the Farrows. Stephanie struggled to concentrate for the remainder of the day. Taking a piece of paper, she wrote out some of her concerns regarding the upcoming camp. Once the list was completed, she realized she had serious reasons to be worried about her clients' safety.

If this camp became a mandatory requirement, she would probably have to resign from her job. How could she possibly stay when she could not support the program? Her only option would be to quit. Then where would she go, and who would care for her clients?

three

"I tell you, Rachel, he's hiding something," Stephanie said to her closest friend as they walked from the apartment kitchen to the living room. Another nagging thought pressed in on her—something about Rachel—but she had been too preoccupied to figure it out.

"That may be, but didn't you say he really knew how to wear a suit?" Rachel giggled as she sat down on Steph's couch and tucked one leg up under her.

"I did?"

Rachel nodded. "I think I should join this desert survival thing. You can have the brawny Mr. Moses, and I'll take the tall, dark, mysterious, well-dressed Mr. Farrow."

"Oh, did I say tall?" A playful grin spread across her face. Before Rachel could respond, the intercom buzzed. "Great. The pizza's here." Stephanie got up to let the deliveryman into the apartment building. Then it dawned on her why Rachel appeared different. "I love your hair, by the way."

"Thanks," Rachel said, patting the blunt ends.

"One Antonio's Supreme without anchovies," a familiar male voice said in the doorway.

Stephanie whirled around. "You! What are you doing here?"

Damian Farrow stood holding a large pizza box and smiling at her. "I met the pizza guy downstairs. I thought I'd pay for your dinner since you wouldn't let me buy lunch." He smiled. "Hope you don't mind."

Rachel jumped up from the couch and came to the door. "Mind? She doesn't mind at all. I'm Rachel Grant." She extended her hand.

"Damian Farrow," he replied, shaking her hand.

Stephanie watched the congenial scene before her, wondering if Rachel had heard anything she'd said only moments before. "Mr. Farrow, how did you get my home address?"

"I'm on several state boards, so I merely called in a favor. Of course, telling the clerk I wanted to send two dozen roses as an apology helped."

How dare he pull a stunt like this? She wondered if she should call the police.

"Well, come in and join us," Rachel offered while Stephanie glared at her.

"I'd like that." He stepped into the living room.

"Can I get you a soda?" Stephanie offered, realizing it was futile to argue at this point.

"Sure. Thanks." Damian seated himself on the couch. "Nice place you have here. I sort of half expected your apartment to be like your office."

"Oh, you mean cluttered." Rachel laughed. "Yeah, you can't move in her office for all the chaos, but this place is stark."

As Rachel and Damian got acquainted, Stephanie went into the kitchen to get a soda for their unexpected guest. Her anger neared the boiling point. She didn't feel threatened by him, but she also didn't trust him. After all, hadn't he admitted he told a lie to get what he wanted?

Damian stayed only a short while. He ate a single slice of pizza and spent most of the visit talking with Rachel. Steph didn't mind; it gave her time to analyze him. She could see he was congenial, educated, and entertaining, once she got past her anger.

"He seems like a nice guy, Steph," Rachel said after Damian left. "What's your problem with him?" She picked up the plates and walked toward the kitchen.

Stephanie followed. "I'm not sure. At least I know he's a liar."

"What? How?"

"He admitted it at the door. Remember?"

"I'd say you're splitting hairs. Maybe he's still going to send the flowers," she said. "He's funny, though."

"Yes, he had a lot of interesting stories to tell, but I thought it strange he never mentioned any incidents at the camp. All Nathan can talk about is that dumb old desert!"

"So it's Nathan now, is it?"

Stephanie swatted the dishcloth at Rachel.

"And as for the camp stories, I'm sure he's heard how you're so totally against this thing, and he didn't want to upset you further."

"I'm not totally against it."

"Yeah, right. Watch out for that bolt of lightning. Did you not hear yourself last weekend? You were determined none of your kids were going to endure a Burning Bush Adventure if you had anything to say about it."

"All right, so I wasn't happy," she admitted.

Rachel laughed. "I think you're confused. That's unusual for you."

"Well, I must confess I'm struggling with my cognitive dissonance."

"Say again?" Rachel frowned.

"It's like this. I *know* this camp is not for my clients, yet I'm trying to justify why they should go."

"So why didn't you say that in the first place?"

Stephanie shrugged.

Leaning on the counter, Rachel asked, "Anyway, what's the problem?"

"Guess I'm worried." She bit her lip pensively. "A lot could go wrong."

"Ever the pessimist, Steph. A lot could go right."

❧

"What time is your first class?" Phil asked from Stephanie's office couch.

"After lunch." She tapped her pen on her blotter.

"Don't look so thrilled," he chided.

"I'm worried," she said, tossing her pen down. "Of the six kids, only two of them seemed even remotely interested in going. I had to twist a lot of arms. Which only proves—well, we won't go there. Will this little outing be mandatory for everyone or just specific cases?"

"That will be up to you and your recommendations."

"Don't try and charm me, Philip James. You already know

my recommendations. I still think you should get someone who actually likes this idea."

"Nah, Steph, this is way better. If Nathaniel Moses can turn you around, I won't even need your report." He chuckled.

"This is way too much fun for you, isn't it?" She walked around to the front of her desk and leaned against it. Seeing Phil flinch, she smiled.

"Yes, I'm rather enjoying it," he answered. "I can't recall when I've seen you so short-fused. It restores my belief that you really are human under all that psychobabble stuff you spout."

"Why, Phil, I had no idea you felt that way," she quipped. "If you don't understand the terms I use, why don't you ask me to explain them?"

"It's not every word."

She leaned toward him. "Now I know what to get you for Christmas. *My First Dictionary.* Perhaps a copy of *Psychology Terms for Dummies,* too."

Phil placed an imaginary check mark on the wall. "Okay, that's one for you."

Stephanie relaxed against the desk, savoring the small victory. "Three, and I get released from this silly camp?"

"Not on your life." He stood and patted her shoulder. "By the way, I don't know if anyone ever told you this, but you can't go hiking around a desert in those." He pointed to her shoes. "That fancy suit and those big floppy things in your ears won't help, either."

"It's only a class."

"Still, I suggest you drop by your place and change into sneakers, jeans, and a T-shirt." He turned to leave, tossing his last words over his shoulder. "You do own such things, don't you?"

Stephanie resisted throwing something at Phil's retreating back. Of course she had such things—somewhere. A quick glance at her watch told her she had time to stop by the sporting goods store to purchase suitable attire for the afternoon.

An hour later she arrived at Burning Bush Adventures. Damian, looking uncomfortable in designer khakis and a linen shirt, stood at the front of the class talking with Nathan. Liz Majors and Heather Downs were already seated. Ever the flirt, Paula Reid leaned over Tom Black's desk, laughing while twisting the earring looped through her lobe. Keith Evans and Ian Parker had yet to arrive.

Stephanie studied Liz's round face and pale blue eyes as the girl smacked her gum. Of all the kids in this group, Liz would be the one she worried about the most. It had surprised Steph that she'd agreed to come. Things must still be bad at home for the girl.

Next, Steph glanced at Heather as she tossed her long, mousy brown hair over her shoulder and watched Paula with envy. *Don't feel bad, Girl; sometimes I wish I were more outgoing like Paula, too.* Steph forced the thought from her mind.

Tom laughed heartily, his white teeth contrasting with his tanned face and dark eyes. He reminded her of a country western singer.

When Stephanie looked away from the kids, she saw Nathan wave her toward him.

Her heart rate quickened as her gaze met his. *Could that be a look of pleasure on his rugged face? Do his eyes look bluer today? Stop it!*

"How was your trip?" she asked when she reached his side. Reassessing his appearance, she noticed his hair seemed a shade lighter, his tan deeper. Being in the desert these last ten days had certainly not made him any worse for wear.

"We had a great time! Two of the guys were from Australia, and they hope to bring back a group next year."

"That's great." She'd had no idea his company attracted clients from that far away.

"Nice to see you dressed for the class, Stephanie," Nathan said as he looked about the room. "Say, do I get to know anything about these kids?"

"Sorry, confidential. I can tell you that none of them are hardened criminals. I only work with first-time offenders who get probation. We feel that early intervention can redirect them down the right path."

"That reminds me of one of my favorite verses in Proverbs," Nathan replied. "I guess the short version would be train a child and he'll always do what's right. You see, a kid needs direction, needs to know the difference between right and wrong. If you show them in the beginning, in the end they'll come back to it." Nathan folded his muscular arms across his broad chest and grinned.

"I don't think it's that simple in this day and age," Stephanie replied.

"Okay, dudes, I'm here. Let the show begin," Keith Evans shouted as he entered the classroom.

Typical, thought Stephanie. Keith hid his inner fears with an outward appearance of bravado and by looking tough in his leather jacket. She recognized his defense mechanism and wouldn't have expected any less of an entrance. Ian Parker, wearing his customary mirror sunglasses, followed Keith in the door.

"I guess we're good to go," Nathan suggested. "If everyone would take a seat—"

"Where am I takin' it to?" Keith asked as he picked up his chair. The group groaned.

"We've got a lot to accomplish in each class, and after that it's no turning back," Nathan continued. "Ten days in the hot desert. You'll never be the same."

❧

"You look positively awful," Rachel greeted as Steph reached the lobby of the theatre.

"Thanks, Rach. You don't look so bad yourself."

"I meant that in the nicest way." Her friend laughed. "Guess the class didn't go so well?"

"Tell me I'm just being a worry wart." Stephanie looked around and found a place to sit. Rachel followed her to a cushioned seat.

"You're just being a worry wart. Feel better?"

"Not exactly."

"Are you going to be able to watch this movie or fret all the way through it?"

Steph sighed. "I know my job, don't I?"

"That's a silly question."

"I know my kids, too, don't I?"

"I think you do a great job with them—despite having your hands tied so often."

Stephanie appreciated the sincere support in Rachel's voice. "So why can't I feel good or bad about this?"

"Huh? Is this that confident dissing thing again?"

Stephanie laughed. "Cognitive dissonance. Yeah, maybe. I know this is a dumb idea and too dangerous. But when I watch Nathan with my kids and see how they respond, I think it's exactly what they need."

"So what's the problem?"

"It's when he starts talking about some of the things they'll be doing, the hazards involved, and the importance of paying attention. I can't help but feel downright ill at the thought of what could go awry."

Rachel glanced at her watch. "So he's rather good with the kids?"

Exasperated, Steph asked, "Didn't you hear anything I said?"

"Of course I did. But you know better than me that building a rapport with the kids is crucial. Not everyone can do it."

"Then tell me why I can't accept this."

"Are you worried the kids will respond to Nathan instead of you?"

"Am I?" She knew the answer before she asked the question. And she didn't need her degree to know why. His comment about emotional distance had been a barb. Every time she thought about it, an ache welled up inside her. *What if he is right?*

"I don't think you need to worry about that," Rachel said.

"I'm not even sure I can last the ten days. I'll be expected to walk over twelve miles a day, carry a heavy pack, and have responsibilities like all of them." Should she mention she couldn't cook?

"You're a survivor. A cynical one, but a survivor. You'll make it. Now let's watch this movie and have some fun."

"I'm glad someone believes in me," Stephanie said, hoping she'd be able to stay focused for the evening.

When the movie ended, they took a walk over to Java Junction for coffee, ordered, and found a table near the window.

"So. Did the handsome Mr. Farrow show for class?" Rachel asked.

"Hmm, let me think. . ." Steph paused and took a sip of her cappuccino. "Yes, I believe he did."

"And?"

"And what?"

"Did he ask about me?"

"Hmm, let me think," she repeated, gazing at the ceiling and tapping a finger against her chin. "Well, he did mention how nice it was to see me again. Then we had to sit down—"

"I didn't ask for a minute-by-minute accounting."

Steph relented with a grin. "Yes, at the end he asked how you were."

"We should have double-dated this evening."

"I think I need a bit of a break from the pressures of trying to get along with those guys."

Rachel giggled. "Damian seems very nice. Nathan, too."

"Yes, Nathan is a nice guy. But *seems* is the operative word for Damian. I don't trust that man. Every time we're together, I can't help but get my hackles up. It's stressful." Steph surprised herself by readily admitting Nathan was nice. A thin ripple of excitement coursed through her.

"No wonder you don't want to spend time in a desert with him."

They both laughed.

"Nathan told the kids they would never be the same after this adventure. I hope that's a good thing."

"You worry too much. What's the worst that could happen out there?"

"I think we've been down this road before. For starters, we could all get heat stroke. Or bitten by animals, some poisonous. Oh, and if I'm leading, we could get turned around in a heartbeat."

"I always said you'd get lost in your own bathroom if we hadn't trained you first."

"Oh, that's empathy, Rachel." Steph faked disgust.

"Don't feel bad. Lots of people are directionally challenged. We still love you."

"Thanks, but that won't get me home safe." She paused. "One of the days will be spent climbing. I'm not looking forward to that, either."

"Did you tell him you're afraid of heights?" Rachel dipped a biscotti into her coffee.

"Of course not. I can't tell him anything. I'll have to grin and bear it. If I so much as whimper once, all the kids will follow suit." Steph lowered her coffee cup.

"You know what?" Rachel asked as she leaned forward. "I'd say you're getting stressed out over nothing. Well, I don't mean nothing," she backtracked, "but you've got eight weeks to get into shape and another seven classes to help you feel comfortable with the goals of the trip."

"And that's the problem. It would appear there are no goals. No structure, no routine." Biting her lip, Steph added, "I wonder what he expects these kids to learn?"

"It sounds to me like the kids aren't the problem."

Steph glared at her. "Low blow, Rachel."

"I'm only trying to help. I'm your friend. Do you trust me to be honest?"

Stephanie hesitated. Of course she trusted Rachel. "You know the answer to that."

"How can you expect your clients to trust you when you can't trust others? Even me, your best, albeit prettier, friend." Rachel smiled.

"I trust people." Perhaps now would be a good time to move before that bolt of lightning zapped her.

"Not enough. I think Nathan wants you and your clients to learn to trust him. And most of all to trust yourselves."

"You may have a point. But I don't think a strenuous trek across a desert is the best way to learn."

"On this outing, Steph, it's not your job to think," Rachel

said with a laugh. "Now c'mon, this is getting too serious. It's Friday night. Let's enjoy ourselves."

Steph appreciated her friend's attempt to lighten the mood, but she felt too overwhelmed to let her thoughts drift far from the upcoming event. What troubled her most was whether she could make the trip. She would lose the respect of her kids if she didn't. And quite possibly the respect of Nathan. Did that matter? If she was honest, it mattered a whole lot.

"Are you listening?"

"Sorry. What did you say?" Steph responded.

"I asked how well the kids got along."

"One of them is a real cut-up. I know he's hiding his true feelings, and I hope he's still paying attention." She thought of how Keith made fun of everything Nathan said. "Two of the girls are quiet, and one of them I fear may cause problems. I have visions of her slipping out at night to be with the guys."

"Too bad you couldn't handcuff them each evening."

"To what? A rock? A sage bush?" Stephanie burst out laughing.

"What's so funny?"

"Nathan explaining that when we leave the others we need to tell them where we're going. The girls were sort of shy, so he told them that the ladies' room in the desert is called the sage bush."

"Oh, I never thought of that. No indoor plumbing."

Steph nodded. "Then Nathan mentioned finding a dead scorpion in his sleeping bag once. I'm going to buy one of those that zip around my head." She shuddered.

"Scorpion or sleeping bag?"

Ignoring her comment, Steph continued. "We're going to learn how to make a still, too."

"I thought you said Nathan didn't drink."

"A water still."

"Too bad. I had visions of you in some tent with Nathan and Damian like a scene out of *M.A.S.H.*"

"You should be going on this trip with us. You don't even have to be in the desert to see a mirage."

"Are you implying something, Stephanie Harris?"

"Never."

"So are you going to sit around all weekend reading whatever it is you read every weekend, or are you going to start getting into shape?"

"I'm going to try to walk two miles tomorrow."

"I thought you had to walk twelve each day?"

"We do, but I can't start out at twelve. I'm starting slow and working my way up."

"You go, Girl. Call me when you're done."

"You mean you're not going to help me?"

"I sit at a computer all day. What do I know about walking? Why, I even order my groceries online and have them delivered."

"There's nothing I can say to convince you to join me?"

"You know me well enough to know there is absolutely nothing you could do, or say, to convince me." Rachel's voice left no room for argument.

"Nothing I can say or do, huh?"

"Right. Nothing."

Steph smiled. "Damian. Date."

"When do we start walking?"

four

"So you do take time to play on the weekends?"

Without looking around she knew who had spoken to her. She felt rather self-conscious being in the one store in town Nathan probably lived in. "Nope. I'm all work." She turned and smiled at him. "I'm picking out my sleeping bag for the trip."

"Don't be swayed by the pretty colored one there. Look for a lightweight, hydrophobic one."

"I'm sorry, but sleeping bags can't have phobias."

He groaned. "Here, this is one of those modular bags like the armed forces use. It weighs less than seven pounds."

"I can read the tag." She scowled at him in mock irritation, willing her heart rate to remain steady.

"What are you doing when you're finished here?"

She pulled out another bag and looked inside it. "I haven't thought that far ahead." She hoped her reply sounded casual.

"Could we go for a coffee?" He leaned against a pillar at the end of the aisle and crossed his arms.

She pushed the sleeping bag back and grabbed another one, trying to read the label. "I'd prefer tea."

He laughed. "Want help with choosing the right equipment?"

"I think I can manage," she said without looking up.

He pushed away from the pillar and turned to leave.

Against her better judgment, she allowed herself to watch Nathan walk away from her. When he looked back and nodded, she felt her face flush. "Oh, he's annoying," she whispered through gritted teeth.

A half hour later, when she left Abner's Sporting Goods, her bank account was a little lighter and her arms a lot heavier.

"Can I help you?"

"If I didn't know any better, Mr. Moses, I'd say you were stalking me."

"Are we back to the Mr. and Miss stuff again?"

He startled her as he reached for one of the bags slipping from her hand.

"Thank you."

"Let me take that other bag, too." He leaned around her and disengaged the handle from her fingers.

She glanced away from his gaze, worried he would ask questions she didn't know how to answer.

They walked silently to her car where she fumbled to open the trunk. He set down the bags and took the keys from her. When the lock clicked, the lid popped open. He took the items from her hand, allowing his gaze to travel up and down her.

She should be annoyed at his overt display, but inwardly she smiled. Already she'd come to realize that he enjoyed life and expressed it fully. A trait that caused her to waffle between jealousy and admiration, and that seemed to bring out the worst in her. She nearly giggled. At least he made her feel *something*.

"So," Nathan began. "I wanted to have a chance to talk with you about our next class and some history of these courses." He closed the trunk and brushed his hands.

"The reason being?"

"I'd like to put your mind at ease. We are at odds over every detail, and that bothers me. I don't want things to stay this way." He paused. "I mean, when we're in the desert."

She nodded for him to continue.

"Will you walk with me around the library grounds?"

"You think we can work out our differences with a leisurely stroll?"

"Something like that." He touched her shoulder in a friendly gesture as they walked together.

A yearning welled up inside her, but she ignored it and tried her best to anger him. "All right then. Let me hear your speech."

"It's not quite that way." He guided her by the elbow as they entered the library grounds. "The great thing discovered through these survival excursions is that anyone can succeed with the right motivation, encouragement, and opportunity. I like to think Burning Bush Adventures provides that exact environment."

"You left out dangerous."

"Sure, there is a bit of danger, perhaps even a pushing of one's limits, but that's only to eradicate the enemy within."

They wandered over to an outdoor water fountain and sat down on the concrete wall. Rays of sunlight glistened off the water. "It all sounds so dramatic. Just what is the enemy within?"

"Fear, defeatism, apathy, and selfishness, to name a few."

"And you can wave a little wand over each of us and remove the nemesis?"

"Nope. Nothing I do on the trip can remove the *nemesis*, as you put it. But it is a learning process. We learn to recognize what is stopping us from succeeding and then overcome the blockade, so to speak. We learn as we go, out in the desert. It's the quickest and most effective way for people to discover how much they depend on each other and how much more they are able to do than they ever imagined."

He spoke with passion, and his handsome face seemed to glow.

She ignored his zeal and watched some children playing nearby. "How so?"

"Like French immersion, where you're thrown into the language totally. You learn or fail."

They were silent for a moment, basking in the sunlight.

"Would it terrify you to be taken to an isolated island, and once you landed, to be told that you had to find your own way back?"

"Of course it would!" She turned to him, worried he might be planning such a trip.

"Don't panic," he said, taking her hands. "I'd never do that to you. But that's what some of the survival camps do. Each of the participants surprised themselves and made it back. What a confidence booster."

"Or a nightmare creator." She pulled from his hold, stood, and began to walk.

Nathan stepped in front of her and gazed into her eyes. She stood still, mesmerized.

"I'll let you in on a little secret," he said. "Most often when a group is out on their own, they are being tracked by experienced guides. The class must work out their route, food, and distance and leave messages twice a day in pre-arranged places. It's not so dangerous, but they don't know that."

A wave of relief washed over her. "So someone will be following—?"

"Look out!" a voice bellowed nearby.

Nathan grabbed Steph's hand and pulled her off the walk, where they tumbled onto the grass. A skateboard whizzed past as a lanky kid fell to the ground beside them.

Nathan pulled her to her feet. "Are you okay?"

She nodded, brushing grass from her clothes.

"Sorry, I didn't realize it sloped so much."

"You're bleeding." Steph reached for the teen's elbow.

He blushed with obvious embarrassment. "Ah, it's nothing."

"Let me take a look."

"I'm fine. I gotta get my board. I'll bet my nose is all scraped up."

"Your nose is fine."

"He means the skateboard, Steph," Nathan said.

"Oh." She watched the boy examine the wheels.

"Any damage?" Nathan asked.

"Nah." The youth dropped the board and jumped onto it. "Sorry," he said as he rolled away.

"Looks like fun, doesn't it? Maybe we should learn to boogie-board."

"Not on your life! I'm not even sure I should be going into the desert."

They started to walk along the path again. "I know a way to build your confidence. At the next class, we'll have the ring of trust. Everyone will stand in a circle with you in the middle. Someone will turn you around and around. When they stop, you will fall back, trusting one of us to catch you."

"We did that sort of thing in college. The moment I chose

to fall, the fire bell rang and everyone ran out."

They laughed together.

"I know you think you can perform miracles," Steph said, "but believing it doesn't make it so. Research shows that your boot camp doesn't work. In fact, a recent study discovered that teaching life skills in elementary school, establishing anti-bullying programs, and rehabilitation programs that work to eliminate illiteracy are far more effective than brute-force programs such as Scared Straight."

Nathan turned her to face him. "Stephanie, I don't run a boot camp," he said, his tone hushed. "In fact, surviving the desert is less traumatic than being sent through one of those programs."

"I'd say they were pretty even."

She could tell he stifled a sigh. "You really have an aversion to this trip, don't you?"

"Now you're beginning to understand." Had she pushed too far? Would a war of words erupt as usual between them? Why did she always provoke him? "There's hope for you yet," she teased and offered him a brief smile.

"I see I've got my work cut out for me."

Thank goodness, he wasn't giving up on her.

They had walked full circle and were back at the beginning. "I need to get going, Nathan. I've got some more errands to run."

"Anything I can help with?"

"No. I'm mad you didn't let me buy the purple sleeping bag. Who cares if the ugly green one weighs less?"

"You will. By the way, who is always complaining about the weight of the packs?"

"Game, set, match."

They strolled in silence back to her car. For an awkward moment neither spoke. "Thanks for spending time with me," Nathan said.

She nodded, and he walked backwards away from her. Clearly neither of them wanted to move on. *You're being so fickle! First you hate the desert, and now it looks pretty inviting! Nothing about the place has changed.* The arid wilderness still contained snakes, scorpions, lizards, and the like. But it would also contain Nathaniel Moses. Which might prove even more dangerous.

❧

"Grab the rope, Liz." Nathan's voice sounded calm while Stephanie's anxiety only heightened.

"I can't," the girl shouted, fear echoing in her words.

Steph, Damian, and the others all stared at the outdoor climbing wall where Liz hung by one hand. Her feet dangled as she screamed for help. Stephanie felt useless waiting on the ground below.

"You can do it," Nathan encouraged from the top. He swung the rope again, to within her grasp.

Ian pulled off his trademark sunglasses, tucked them into a pocket, and started up the wall. "Liz, I'm right below you! I've got ahold of the rope. Just reach a little to your left. Don't look down."

"A bit more, Liz, and you've got it," Nathan said.

Liz reached for it, lost her hold, and screamed as she began to fall.

"Grab it!" Ian bellowed.

Nathan pulled up on the line in the same moment Liz clenched her fist tightly around the rope. "You all right?"

"No!" she screamed.

"Stay there, Liz." Nathan began to work his way down the gray imitation mountain.

"Hang on, I'm right below you," Ian said. "I can push your foot into one of the holds." He reached up, grabbed her left foot, and placed it into position. "Give me a sec while I move up closer."

Liz stared down, still holding tightly to the rope. When Ian got close enough, he put her other foot into a nearby hold. As he moved up the wall to Liz's side, they could hear him ask, "You okay?"

Stephanie finally let out her breath. She wiped her sweaty palms on her jeans and hoped no one could see her reaction.

"That was an amazing maneuver you made to get that

rope," Nathan said, sounding like a proud parent when he reached Liz's side. "How are your hands?"

Stephanie clenched her teeth while Liz responded to Nathan's question. This was exactly the type of event that caused all her fears. And they were still merely in class.

"I—I'm not s—sure how much longer I can h—hold on," she stuttered. Tears slipped down her cheeks.

"I'll help you back down. But first you need to let go of the rope and get your hands back into the holds. Can you do that for me?" Nathan's voice could barely be heard. Ian rubbed Liz's shoulder in a gesture of comfort.

Ian's actions surprised Stephanie. She hoped she'd remember later to make a note of it in his file.

With the help of Nathan and Ian, Liz managed to make it down without further incident.

"Are you all right?" Stephanie gave Liz a brief hug.

"I think so."

"What happened?"

"I don't know. I guess I panicked. But Nathan, I mean, Mr. Moses and Ian really helped. I didn't think I could get back down. But I did!"

"Who's next?" Nathan shouted as he readied the rope.

Tom stepped forward.

"Don't you think they should be attached to the rope?" Stephanie asked as she glared at Nathan.

"On a small practice wall like this with all the padding below? Nope."

Did the man not understand he was playing with people's lives? "I don't think it's safe."

"It's safer here than in the desert."

"Liz could have been hurt."

"She may have been frightened but not hurt. Stunt men fall into that stuff all the time from much higher heights." He moved toward the wall. "Besides, it's better if she falls here than fifty miles away from help and without the cushion below."

"I'm fine, Miss Harris, really I am. Nathan says we'll always have the rope on out in the desert." Liz's voice still trembled as she defended him.

"If you have a problem with anything, Miss Harris, please discuss it with me later," Nathan said. "Okay, Tom, you're up."

"Not quite," he replied, pulling a long blade of grass from his mouth and tossing it down. He placed his hands in the holds and started to climb.

Stephanie could feel the anger rise within her. How dare he chastise her in front of the group like that? But at the same time, how dare she question him in front of everyone?

"Miss Harris, it's okay," Liz said, interrupting her thoughts. "I'm fine. My hands are a little sore, but they'll heal. I want to do this."

"Let me see." She reached over and studied Liz's palms. They didn't look too bad, after all. "I've got some lotion in the car. I'll get it for you."

Liz followed Stephanie, all the while talking about how frightened she had been at first but now wanted to try it again. They stood by the car, chatting for a few minutes.

The girl's resilience surprised Steph. "Liz, what do you hope to gain by this experience?"

"I don't know, really." She popped a piece of gum into her mouth.

"Why did you want to come?"

"I needed to get away from—" She stopped.

Stephanie waited.

Liz looked away. "I needed a bit of a break."

"So you'd rather sleep in a cold desert at night, hike in the heat by day, and ruin your beautiful hands climbing than be at home?"

Liz nodded, then grinned. "So why are you coming?"

"Because. . ." Stephanie hesitated. She couldn't very well say because she had no choice. How would that look to the kids? "I wanted to make sure this was the right thing for all of you."

"But look at your lovely nails. You'll have to cut them before we leave."

Steph hadn't thought about that. *Oh, well, they grow fast,* she consoled herself. "You guys are worth it," she replied and meant it.

Together, they walked back to the practice wall. Tom had made it to the top and back down, and Heather had already climbed halfway up.

"It works better if you *open* your eyes," Keith offered.

"I can't," Heather yelled.

"You're almost to the top. Do you want to go back down?" Nathan asked her.

"No, all the way."

"You don't have to do this," Stephanie called up to her.

Heather didn't reply.

Arrggghh, I knew I was right. She'll force herself to do this because of the peer pressure. "Heather, I'm ordering you to come down now."

"Miss Harris, she's doing fine." Nathan's words were clipped, and she could tell his patience had reached its limit.

"Look, she made it!" cheered Paula, who stopped twisting her earring long enough to applaud.

Heather opened her eyes and looked around. "Wow! I can see for miles."

Liz leaned over to Stephanie and whispered, "We'll let you know when we've had enough. Then you can defend us, okay?"

Stephanie laughed. "All right, Liz."

Once everyone else had made the climb, it was Steph's turn. She looked at the wall, glanced around at the students and Damian, then rested her gaze on Nathan.

"Ready?"

"Of course, Mr. Moses."

"Good. Here we go." He started up the wall ahead of her.

She stuffed her hand into the first hold and pulled it back in one swift movement. Pain shot through her little finger, and she grasped it tightly. After a few seconds she looked at it. The long nail had broken down to the nail bed.

"Ouch. That's gotta hurt," Keith said, staring at her finger as blood pooled under the pink polish.

"Are you coming?" Nathan waited just above her.

"Hang on." She pulled a tissue from her pocket, wrapped the nail, and tried again.

When she reached the top, she paused. She felt exhilarated and awed. "It's so lovely!"

"Wait 'til you see it in the desert."

She turned to look at him. He smiled at her.

"I'm glad you like it. I ordered this view just for you. Look over there." He pointed eastward to the orange and purple sky.

"It takes my breath away."

"Mine, too." His voice sounded wistful.

When she looked over at him, his intense blue eyes were on her.

❧

It had been six weeks since their first practice climb and tonight, to Steph's relief, all had gone well. Even Damian had become fairly adept. Now they were back in the classroom. Stephanie struggled to pay attention to Nathan.

"That seems like too much water." Tom's words brought her out of her reverie.

"Actually, you'll need to use it with caution. It's better to drink small amounts constantly than to go without as long as you can and then guzzle. Water is heavy to carry, and as I said before, we plan our route from oasis to oasis. Just about the time we need more water, we should be near some."

"Won't the water be yucky?" Paula asked.

"If we come upon any spoiled water, we'll boil it. Your packs will contain iodine tablets to treat the water first."

"Has anyone ever not made it out of one of these trips?" Liz queried from the back of the room.

"Not on my group. I think, a few years back, some people left the core and headed out on their own. One didn't survive. But we shouldn't have any problems."

Stephanie squirmed inwardly when Nathan's eyes rested on her. She looked about the room and wondered why Damian had been so quiet all evening. While she still distrusted the guy, he'd been pretty good to the kids. Maybe it was because she'd done a little checking up on him. His name seemed synonymous with generosity—a fact that surprised her. Perhaps it was because of his father's philanthropic reputation. She would remain cautious all the same.

"You said we all have to cook. I'm never any good at that. What if everyone gets sick?" Paula asked while playing with the gold hoop in her ear.

"We don't let you cook anymore," Keith quipped.

Nathan chuckled. "You'll do fine. Remember, the first rule here is not to anticipate problems and panic."

"Yeah, there'll be plenty without our anticipating more," Keith chided again.

You took the words right out of my mouth, Steph thought.

"At least we know we'll be well entertained," Ian said.

The small group laughed.

"If things get out of hand, we can use Miss Harris's cell phone and call for a ride home." Tom flashed her a grin.

"I don't know where I'd charge the thing," Steph said, finally joining the conversation.

Nathan laughed. "Now, any more questions?"

Everyone shook their heads.

"Then we're done for today. You've got four days to practice the knots, do your daily stretching exercises, and rest up. This time next week, we'll be almost halfway through our trek across the desert. See you at four A.M. Tuesday!"

Stephanie remained seated as the kids milled around and talked with Nathan. Damian looked over at her and smiled, then headed her way.

"How do you think this little excursion will turn out?"

"I'm hopeful but hesitant," she replied.

"Seems like the kids like you. They'll depend on you to be their ally."

Ally? Why would they need one? "Just like you and Nathan." She felt certain his comment contained a hidden meaning, but she ignored the feeling.

"Indeed."

"Well, I guess I'd better get going. I've got to stop by the office and pick up some work. Have a nice weekend, Damian."

"Maybe I'll run into you and Rachel."

"She'd like that."

Nathan came up to her as she headed out the door. "Can we have dinner one night before we leave?"

"Sure. Give me a call," she answered, wishing he had wanted to see her tonight.

"I'm looking forward to it."

For some reason, so was she.

❧

After everyone had gone, Nathan sat down at his desk to sort out his monthly expenses. He could feel a wrenching in his gut as he considered the need for this government contract. Agreeing to eight weeks of classes had severely hampered his ability to take another group out.

Plus, business had been unusually slow prior to this, and now his savings were nearly depleted. Providing a camp each month for first-time offenders seemed like a gift from God. Would it be enough to keep his doors open? Then, when word got out about his success, major businesses would begin contacting him for short survival and teamwork trips. Finally, all his hard work—and prayers—would pay off.

But first he had to get past the appealing, yet annoying, Stephanie Harris.

"That girl has problems," he said aloud, shaking his head. Problems he knew he'd love to help her with. If only she'd retract her claws long enough for him to get near her. He laughed at the thought. She did smile at him at the top of the wall, and he found himself being drawn to her. But becoming involved with her was not an option.

He marveled at her determination to protect her clients and her ability to feign strength. Everything about her seemed mysterious yet inviting. He'd never met a woman who caused such a commotion in his heart and head. More than anything, he needed to keep his distance. He must win Stephanie's approval fairly, as well as the contract. It was the only thing that would save his business and ensure he kept his promise.

So much seemed to be at stake, and Nathan wondered if

he would be able to keep a tight rein on his feelings for the petite blonde who invaded his thoughts at every turn.

A sudden noise caught his attention. He looked around. "What brings you back here?"

Damian seated himself nearby. "I wanted to discuss a few things before we leave for the desert."

Nathan rested his hands behind his head and leaned back in his chair. "Shoot."

"I'm still worried about that scene with Liz the first time at the climbing wall."

"How so?"

"I think there'll be problems out in the desert."

"I disagree, Damian. Even if she had fallen, she wouldn't have been hurt."

"That's not what I meant. Miss Harris seemed determined to put a stop to things."

"She's all right. A little overprotective, maybe, but all right."

"A little. I don't know what her problem is, but I'm worried how it will affect your business. I wanted to reassure you that I'll put in a good word for you. I've got a date with her this weekend. I'm sure I can convince her to ease off a bit."

Nathan stiffened at Damian's words, surprised at how they irked him. Stephanie had agreed to join him for dinner before Tuesday. Now, as he recalled the conversation, he realized he had not been clear as to when they would get together. If Damian wanted Stephanie, Nathan felt he didn't have a chance against the educated fast-talker. Damian certainly seemed more her type. Any woman in her right mind would pick luxury over rustic.

"I'll let you know how it goes." Damian winked at Nathan.

"Not interested."

Damian flinched, but the slight obviously didn't deter him. "When are we going to discuss our partnership?"

Nathan could be patient no longer. "Why do you want in on this so badly?" As he spoke, he realized his business was just like a marriage. He would never marry a non-Christian. Why would he consider a partnership with one? *Thank You,*

Lord, for showing me this. I'll tell him now.

"It has great potential." Damian stood and started pacing. "I believe I could bring in the business, and you could drag them all out to that hot, barren land. We could make a lot of money."

Nathan wanted to tell Damian there would be no such partnership, no money, but he felt God's prompting to wait. "Maybe it should be reversed. I'll bring them in; you train them. You've got the education."

Damian laughed, but Nathan remained straight-faced. "You know far more than me about training them—without a degree."

"You'll learn a lot starting next week." *Okay, Lord, I guess he's coming with us. I don't know why, but I'm trusting You.*

five

"I'll be glad when this survival camp is over and we can get back to our regular fun conversations," Rachel said as she dipped her taco chip in the hot salsa.

The new restaurant's lively rock music pounded in their ears while they ate. Exhausted from the week, Steph had wanted to bail on their standing Friday night "date." She poured more diet cola from the carafe into her glass. "I still have some reservations, that's all," she said, hoping she didn't sound defensive.

"Didn't you say that one of the guys jumped right in to help when the girl had problems on the climbing wall?"

"Ian and Liz. He sure impressed me with how calm he remained. Liz is great at climbing now."

"See, that's the cup-half-full side of the event. You're too busy looking at the cup-half-empty side."

"Tell me again why we're friends?" Stephanie said with a pout.

Rachel laughed. "I'm serious. You've got to change your perspective on life. How you managed to get a degree in psychology with such a jaded view on things is beyond me."

"Leave the analyzing for me."

"Yeah, I'm not getting paid, so why should I care?"

Steph took a bite of her chip before answering. "Now who's the pessimist?"

"Did you talk to Damian today?"

"Yes. He said he hoped to see you this weekend. I told him it would have to be after our ten-mile walk tomorrow."

Rachel groaned. "Oh, Stephanie, not tomorrow. I'm still tired from our last walk—and that was only eight miles. I can't do it."

"Your heart will really thank me if you do."

"You just want to make a good impression on this Nathan guy."

"You think my love life is more important than my clients or my dearest friend?"

"All right, I'll walk with you tomorrow."

"Good evening, ladies," Damian said as he approached their table. "Mind if I join you?"

"Not at all," Rachel quickly replied, scooting over to make room for him.

Steph resisted the urge to ask him to leave. Didn't the man have a life? Why was he always showing up wherever she went? Yes, it was a relatively small community, but until recently she'd never traveled in the same circles as the great Mr. Farrow. What had changed?

He seated himself beside Stephanie. "So in four days we'll be out in the middle of nowhere."

"I'd prefer to forget about that for now," Steph replied.

"We haven't ordered yet. Do you want to join us, or do you have plans?" Rachel asked.

"I'd like nothing better than to spend my evening with two of the most beautiful women in town." Damian leaned back to gain the attention of a nearby waitress and ordered a drink. "So tell me, Stephanie, what did you think of today's lesson?"

She didn't want to be rude, but she had already made it clear she wasn't in the mood to discuss the day's events, nor next week's. "When I'm at work, I discuss work," she said.

Rachel glared at her. "Well, what Stephanie means is that when she's enjoying herself, she doesn't like to be reminded of her difficult job."

"I understand totally." Damian nodded in Stephanie's direction, leaning over and patting the back of her hand.

Pulling away from his touch, she smiled weakly at him. "I appreciate it."

"What do you do in your spare time?" Rachel asked Damian.

"I like fast cars and horses."

And probably fast women, Stephanie wanted to add.

"I guess that's quite the contrast to hot, slow days in the desert." Rachel leaned closer and smiled.

While the two of them chatted on, Stephanie drifted off

into her own thoughts. It seemed strange to her that Damian would be interested in either one of them. He was a smooth talker with expensive clothes. On the other hand, she found herself thinking of Nathan far too often, and he was the athletic, outdoor type. *Guess it's true that opposites attract.*

Glancing around the room, she thought she saw Nathan leaving the restaurant. Had he been here? Why didn't he come over? Perhaps he wasn't in the mood for her sharp tongue this evening. *Why do I talk to him like that?*

"What do you think?" Rachel asked.

"Hmm, what?" She slowly broke from her daze.

"Damian invited us to his home for a dip in the pool tomorrow afternoon."

"That's nice," Stephanie said.

"Will you excuse us, Damian? We need to visit the ladies' room to freshen up," Rachel said. Damian stood instantly, and Rachel grabbed Steph's hand and dragged her.

"What's the matter, Rachel?" Steph asked once they were far enough away from the table.

"Where were you out there?"

"I don't know. I guess I'm tired. It's been a long week. Why don't I make my excuses and leave you and Damian to enjoy dinner together."

"You'd do that for me?" Rachel asked as they entered the restroom.

Steph took a seat on the small bench. "That's what friends are for. I'm a third wheel. Here's some money for my soda. You two have a good time."

"Hey, what am I thinking?" Rachel checked herself in the mirror. "We agreed we'd never let a guy come between our friendship. We always go out together on Friday nights."

"So this one time, we won't. It's no big deal. You'll have more fun with him tonight anyway." Stephanie hugged Rachel.

"Thanks! I owe you. He's so interesting and fun. Can you believe he owns this place?"

Steph blinked in surprise. "He does?"

"See, I knew you weren't paying attention."

"Go on." She motioned for Rachel to leave. "Have fun. Call me tomorrow."

Rachel offered a quick wave and was gone.

Stephanie could tell by her friend's bounce that she was falling for Damian, and an ill feeling washed over her. Who was this guy? With all his money and resources, why open such a place? This town needed another eatery like a centipede needed more legs.

She slipped out of the restaurant. The evening air felt refreshing, and she was relieved to be free of the noisy building. Feeling weary, she headed straight home. All she wanted was her nice, comfortable bed and about fifteen hours of sleep.

❧

Nathan had spotted the new restaurant earlier while out jogging. He'd come back this evening to try the food. Seeing Damian and Stephanie seated together, with another woman, was an unexpected shock. Though Damian had said he would be having dinner with Steph, Nathan hadn't believed him. *Why are you so jealous?* He knew why. Stephanie Harris got to him like no other woman. She irritated him, annoyed him, and got him hot under the collar worse than any desert could.

Lord, what do I do about this? How can I spend ten days with this creature? You're going to have to work a miracle to keep my mind on the job.

While he struggled with his thoughts, he left the restaurant wondering what type of game Damian was playing. Surely there must be a reason he suddenly wanted to be partners.

Had he heard that Stephanie would be considering his camp? If so, how? Even *he* didn't know until the last minute. In fact, he'd been informed he would be dealing with Philip James. Of course, Stephanie was probably much better looking—and much more work.

I'm trusting You, Lord. If I'm not to get out of this business, I'll expect You to help me. You know I could live out there forever and never complain a bit. But I'll do as you ask.

He missed the beauty of the desert. But when he closed his eyes, all he could see was Stephanie's pretty face with her luminous green eyes and soft, inviting smile. In his vision, he saw her break into laughter, and the sight warmed him through like a mug of hot chocolate on a cool night. He resisted his feelings. Until everything was sorted out with his business, he needed to keep his distance from her. Even then he would still need to stay clear. She wasn't a Christian, and he knew all too well the pain of loving someone with whom he couldn't share his faith. Yes, Stephanie would have to be kept at arm's length.

Then he remembered the moment atop the climbing wall. That special moment when their eyes met. He had felt like he was falling—an eerie sensation, yet somehow desirable. He pushed all thoughts of Stephanie from his mind and started to pray. He needed guidance and he needed it fast. Starting Tuesday, they would be in close quarters twenty-four hours a day. How would he survive?

&

Bleary-eyed and grumpy, Stephanie wheeled her car into the parking lot. The sky, not yet awake either, remained dark. In the beam of the trailer's lights, she spotted Nathan. Nine stacks of miscellaneous items such as firewood, water jugs, and food stood like little soldiers in front of the long vehicle.

Damian stood nearby, idly drinking something hot while steam escaped the lid. Leaving her stuff in the car for now, she got out and went directly to Nathan.

"Good morning," he greeted cheerfully then frowned.

She ignored his facial expression. "I think good night is more appropriate."

"You're leaving?"

"No, but it's certainly not morning."

Nathan snickered. "Ah, Miss Harris, I think you may have been late to class the day we discussed proper attire."

She felt the blood rise to her cheeks. "This is a very appropriate outfit." And expensive, she wanted to add. On top of that, the khaki shorts, jacket, and T-shirt totally lacked the ability to coordinate with anything else in her closet.

"Shorts are prohibited. Loose-fitting pants provide better air circulation and protection."

She couldn't help but notice as his eyes looked up and down her bare legs. *If I make it back from this trip, I'll shoot that man myself,* she promised. "I'll slip into the classroom and change, if that's all right with you." *I don't care if it is, either.*

She bit her bottom lip and marched back to her car. After fumbling for a few minutes, she gathered everything and went inside the trailer. When she stepped out of the classroom, she saw Nathan nod at her now covered legs.

"Much better, Miss Harris."

Was he blushing? "Thank you." She brushed a fleck of dust off her cotton twill pants.

"We only need two vehicles, since six of us can fit in the Burr."

"Excuse me?"

"That's my name for the Suburban over there." Nathan pointed as he spoke.

Steph nodded. "I thought you had a jeep."

"That's for running around town. I take the Burr to the desert."

"Ah. Well, we can take my sedan. I don't mind." Mentally she thought about whether she had enough gas, then wondered why Damian hadn't offered his vehicle.

"Normally I'd offer my Tahoe, but I just had it detailed," Damian said, as if reading her thoughts.

"I don't mind."

Before the conversation could continue, the kids started to arrive. It seemed obvious right away who had the same morning disposition as Steph. Liz and Ian barely had their eyes open, while Paula looked as if she had been sucking on a lemon. Keith came bounding in behind them, slapping everyone on the back in a friendly greeting. Tom was his usual quiet self. The early morning didn't seem to be a hardship for him.

"Hey, Stephanie, got a question for you," Keith said.

"What?"

"I was reading some books about the desert last night and wondered what they called camels without any humps?"

"You mean a camel with only one hump instead of two?"

She didn't quite understand his question.

"A camel without any hump would be a horse," Damian said sourly.

"Oh, I thought you'd call it Humphrey."

Several of them groaned.

"No time for games, gang," Nathan said. "Let's get everything loaded. Your names are on the packs, and each of you needs to pick a pile there and make it all fit. Did everyone bring their sleeping bags?"

A murmur of "yeses" echoed in the quiet morning as one by one they began working.

"What's the number-one rule?" Nathan asked as lifted his pack.

"Don't anticipate problems," they said in unison.

"What's the most important item in your pocket?"

"I don't have any pockets," Keith answered.

"Lip balm," Paula said, licking the colored coating on her lips.

"Is there such a thing as quicksand?"

Silence.

Stephanie stifled a laugh. "I don't think we covered that, Nathan."

"It was just a trick question. You'll find out when we get there." He turned away and then shouted, "Move 'em out."

This was it. No turning back. Fear rose in her throat as Stephanie climbed into her car. Liz, Keith, and Ian piled in after her. As they moved farther from town, following the Burr, a small rumble of excitement stirred in her stomach. Maybe it was only hunger.

The predawn morning began to blossom with incredible hues. In a short time, the sky would turn bright, as if a navy dome had been lifted from overhead, exposing the world to light.

She shivered.

Were her fears grounded? Would they survive the next ten days or not?

❧

"Let's have some tunes," Keith suggested as they drove along.

"Sure, what do you want to sing?" Stephanie deliberately misinterpreted his request.

"Don't quit your day job, Miss H.," he teased her. "A comedienne you ain't!"

"Wouldn't think of it, Keith. I'd miss you." She glanced at him in the rearview mirror just as he placed his sunglasses over his eyes.

"So what do you think of all this?" He didn't direct his question to anyone in particular.

Stephanie remained silent, waiting for someone to voice their opinion.

"Well, I think I've learned a lot," Liz said tentatively.

"I think I'm looking forward to it." Ian's words also lacked conviction.

"I worry we'll destroy something," Liz sighed. "Mr. Moses kept saying, 'We're not out there fighting the desert, but becoming a part of it, appreciating it, surviving it.'"

"I'm sure you'll do fine—we'll all do fine." Stephanie hoped she sounded believable.

"I wanna see rattlers, Gila monsters, geckos, and what's the name of that lizard that shoots blood from its eyes?"

Stephanie cringed at Ian's comment. *You're really helping here!*

"I'd like to see a kangaroo rat."

"I agree, Liz, he looked so cute in the picture." *Hope he's as cute in real life.*

A little after seven, they arrived at their destination. Before them in almost every direction lay vast, dry land.

At first glance, nothing here warranted the love and passion Nathan displayed when talking about this place. She worried that by the end of ten days she'd never want to see Nathaniel Moses or his beloved desert again.

This thought bothered her, and she quickly chased it from her mind, reminding herself not to anticipate problems. Great. Now she even sounded like him!

"Okay, we'll get the Burr unloaded first." Nathan's words intruded on her thoughts. "Everyone find your packs. Here's the duty roster. Once we're unloaded and ready to go, our guide will direct us."

"Aren't you our guide?" Paula asked.

"I believe Tom is our guide today," he answered her then turned to Tom. "We'll give you a few minutes to study the map, and then when you're ready, let us know."

Stephanie watched as Tom gulped and began working with the others to unload the vehicle.

"Ian, you'll be responsible for dinner this evening."

"Oh, no!" Keith groaned.

"What is it?" Stephanie asked, worried something was already wrong.

"I forgot my antacids if he's cooking." Keith ducked as Ian attempted to swat him with his hat.

Nathan ignored the antics. "Are we ready?"

"Aye, aye," Keith retorted with a salute.

"This is it. It's been a pleasure to have you all in my class, and I hope this practical exercise will only be an extension of the last eight weeks. I expect each of you to respect the land and your fellow survivalists, as well as yourselves. I don't want to hear the words 'I can't,' but I never grow tired of hearing the words 'thanks for your help, Man.' " He paused, looked around at each of them, and then continued. "See this whistle?" He pulled a silver chain out from under his shirt.

"If at any point you feel you can't continue, grab this whistle and blow it with all your might."

Stephanie wanted to snatch it from Nathan right now, but fear kept her feet rooted to the dusty ground.

"Remember, this is not a competition in any way. Above all else, be true to yourself. Never underestimate your ability to succeed."

"Has anyone ever blown the whistle?" Heather asked timidly.

"Never."

Stephanie watched as the color drained from the girl's face.

Nathan must have seen it, too, for he quickly added, "That doesn't mean no one wanted to. But they faced their fear and got the job done. We're here to support each other. I don't anticipate anyone needing to blow it."

Stephanie felt uncomfortable with the way the conversation had veered. She cleared her throat and tried to speak calmly. "Don't hesitate to talk to someone about your feelings, okay?"

Heather nodded, and Nathan continued with a few more last-minute instructions. "Okay, gang, let's have a moment of reflective thought."

The minute seemed like hours to Stephanie, the silence almost unbearable to her. When she finally glanced up, she saw Keith pull off his hat, place it over his heart, and sing, "I can see clearly now the rain—"

Ian cuffed him lightly up the back of the head. "Knock it off. You're scaring all the animals away with that croaking."

Nathan locked the Burr, tucked the keys into his pocket, and asked, "Where's our guide?"

Tom hesitantly stepped forward. He slung his heavy pack over his shoulders and smiled sheepishly at Stephanie. She returned a reassuring grin and stepped in behind him as he led off. The ground crunched in rhythmic sounds beneath their feet as the others followed.

In many ways, the noise was soothing for Steph. Like being in a car with the constant hum relaxing her into drowsiness.

It would be midday before they stopped to rest. She tried not to think about that being so far away. The chatter had died down dramatically, and the awakening desert echoed in the already oppressive air. The sky glowed a perfect cloudless blue, in stark contrast to the brown earth below it.

Alone with her thoughts, Stephanie lagged back from the frontline. She watched Nathan as he marched along with a large wooden staff in his hand. To her it seemed like some sort of flagpole he would plant in the soil when they arrived at their destination, like an astronaut on the moon. After all, wasn't the desert as bleak and barren as the moon?

Damian ambled up beside her, breaking her reverie.

"He makes it sound like it's tough out here."

"It is."

"Not with me around. I'll make sure everyone gets back in one piece."

"Isn't that your job?" Stephanie watched as Damian flinched at her words.

"Yeah, it is."

"They appear to be getting into this, so I hope all goes well."

Damian nodded. "These kids seem fine the way they are. I think Nathan's desperate need for consistent income—like a government contract—is the only reason he's pushing this. I'm certain if he can't get that, he'll be out of business."

His words forced all the air from her lungs. Could he be right? "Frankly, Mr. Farrow, I don't think it's proper for you to discuss your financial matters with me," she said through taut lips.

"Oh, yes, you're quite right. Forgive me."

You're a weasel of a man. And she had no intention of forgiving him. He had a reason for his comments, and she felt sure it was not a commendable one.

❧

Nathan awoke first the next morning. Pulling a small two-way radio from his pack, he contacted his "adventure" friend Jim and advised all was well. On longer treks, Nathan would not only report in daily, but Jim would fly over and drop additional food and supplies as needed. With this short excursion, however, such a flight would not be required. Nathan knew Jim would still fly by once or twice to make sure everything was okay, and he appreciated the man's concern.

Placing the radio back in his pack, he pulled out his Bible. *Thank You, Lord, for getting us through day one.* He opened the book and began to read. Soon he found he couldn't stay focused.

His thoughts returned to Stephanie. He felt bad every time he remembered the embarrassment on her face when he told her to change clothes. He hadn't meant to hurt her feelings. *Why can't I relate to that woman? I'm always saying the wrong things.*

"Good morning." Steph's unexpected whisper from behind startled him. She took a half step backward, eyes wide.

"Yes, it is." He tried to recover gracefully.

She giggled—a beautiful sound. "I wasn't sneaking up on you. I was just trying to be quiet since the others are still sleeping."

"Understandable," he mumbled. *How could anyone look so lovely first thing in the morning?*

"Yesterday was pretty long. How do you think the kids are doing?"

"I think they're doing great. So are you." Of course, he knew it always started out this way.

"I had fun." She sat down and rubbed her foot, then pulled off her sock to examine it.

"Got a problem?"

She glanced down at her foot. Even in the early-morning light, he could see the soft burn in her pretty face. "A blister. I'll be fine."

He went over to the first-aid kit and then came back. Bending down in front of her, he lifted her foot and tenderly rubbed some ointment into the open wound. Without a word, he covered it with a bandage and returned the medication to the case.

"I'm worried. Yesterday was a rather long day," Steph said.

"So you already mentioned," he answered lightly. "They'll survive."

"Sometimes I don't think you understand how difficult life is for them."

Was this a challenge? He waited a moment before answering. "Sometimes struggles can be good things. If everything was handed to us, we wouldn't appreciate it, would we?" He regretted the harshness of his tone. *Lord, she's doing it to me again. How can she be so wonderful one moment and so annoying the next?*

"I'm not in disagreement with that principle. But most of these kids have nothing. While I can't go into the details of their home life, suffice it to say it isn't a picnic."

"None of us have led pain-free lives, Stephanie, and this excursion is a different type of pain. Sure, it's physical, but there's a lot to gain here. When you strip away the blisters, sunburns, cuts, and scrapes, they'll walk away stronger, better people. Able to face each day and any challenge as adults."

"Except for the fact that they are not adults, and they have plenty of time to grow up and learn about themselves. Why should it be force-fed to them in ten days?"

Nathan picked up his Bible. *Lord, help me.* "I understand your concern," he said. "At the first sign of trouble, we'll pull out. I promise."

Before Stephanie could reply, the others began to stir. He watched her face, drinking in her natural beauty, then set to work detailing the day. He found it hard to keep his eyes off her and prayed no one would notice.

The morning went quickly with Keith leading. Every time Stephanie broke out into laughter, Nathan yearned to be closer to her. It seemed like a very long time before they stopped for lunch.

"Liz, I think you need some more sunscreen and lip balm," Nathan said as he sat on their rolled sleeping bags. No one dared to sit on the scorching ground.

"Got it right here, Uncle Nate."

Keith had started the nickname Liz used, and though he pretended to wince when they said it, Nathan kind of enjoyed the endearment. "That's what I like to see." He smiled at her.

"Are you going to tell us another story, Uncle Nate?" Keith asked through a mouthful of food.

"Yep, part of the requirements." He smiled at the group.

Everyone laughed.

"Look around at each other," he began. "And tell me what you see."

"A lot of red faces," Tom offered.

"Does my hair look as bad as Paula's?" Heather sounded whiney and tired.

"Worse," Keith said.

"Okay, I'm serious here." Nathan regained their attention. "Ian, look at Keith. What do you see?"

Ian lowered his mirror sunglasses. "A cut-up."

Nathan glared at him.

"Okay, I think I see a rich kid trying hard to be like everyone else. I think all his humor is a defense."

"Keith, your turn. What do you see when you look at Ian?"

"A guy who obviously needs to keep those glasses on."

The group chuckled.

Again, Nathan leveled his gaze.

"I see someone wishing he was rich like me."

Ian stood, but before he could do much Nathan jumped in between the two guys.

"This is not an insult match. So cool it. Now, Tom, what do you see when you look at Miss Harris?" He didn't want to draw her into this, but he hoped it would defray the tension for a moment.

"I see a neat freak who won't admit it. She's horrified with the bad hair day she's having."

Nathan smiled as he watched Stephanie try to smooth back her blonde waves with her hands.

"Heather, your turn. Look at Paula," Nathan directed.

"I see someone I think pretends to be a dumb blonde." Both girls glared at each other.

"Good, Heather. Contrary to popular belief, this wasn't an exercise in brutal honesty," Nathan said as he returned to his seat. "So one day, a shabby-looking couple walked into the office of the president of Harvard University, and his secretary could tell right away that her boss wouldn't be interested in seeing these people.

"But no matter what the secretary said, they insisted on waiting. She could not get rid of the country bumpkins." Nathan moved around as he spoke and smiled inwardly when all eyes followed him.

"Once she realized their determination, she had the president come out and see them. The lady told him their son had attended Harvard but was accidentally killed about a year ago. They wanted to build a memorial to him somewhere on the campus." Nathan paused. "What do you think was the president's response?"

"He told them the students would welcome their moonshine still?" Keith slapped his knee as he laughed.

"He probably laughed at them," Heather said timidly.

Nathan glanced at Stephanie, who looked away quickly. "The president replied that they couldn't build a statue for every person who attended Harvard and died. And he didn't say it in the nicest way, either."

"I'll bet," interjected Damian in his usual sour tone. His attitude was beginning to annoy Nathan.

"The lady quickly corrected the president by telling him they didn't want to erect a statue. They wanted to donate a building. Of course, the old president's patience was wearing thin, so he asked them if they had any idea how much a building cost, and before they could answer, he set them straight.

"He was mighty pleased with himself when the woman shut right up. He figured he could get rid of these losers and get back to work now."

"But?" Liz asked.

Nathan smiled. "Well, the woman turned to her husband and said, 'Is that all it costs to start a university? Why don't we build our own?' They graciously thanked the president for his time and left."

Paula looked at Nathan with confusion. "What was the purpose of that story?"

"I'm not done yet. Anyone know who those poor-looking people were?"

Everyone shook their heads.

"Mr. and Mrs. Leland Stanford. Their university in California is a memorial to their son." Nathan walked over to his backpack. "Who would have guessed? They looked so poor, so uneducated. And both the secretary and the president judged them by what they saw."

"I still say I saw Ian wishing he was rich like me," Keith said.

"Yeah, right, Man." Ian folded his arms across his chest.

Nathan could tell the teen wished he had a snappy comeback. "Hang on, guys. All of us allow first impressions and outward appearances to sway us. And it's not just with people. When you look out into this vast area you may think, hey, how hard can it be? It's flat. But don't be fooled by appearances. It may look safe and seconds later you're drowning in a flash flood, stuck in quicksand, or worse. Keep your eyes open, listen to your intuition, and never judge by appearances."

"Tell us another story, Uncle Nate!" the kids shouted.

"Nope. There's work to be done. We'll rest here until it cools down a bit. Keith, we'll go over the map to ensure we make it to the first oasis tonight. If anyone has any problems or questions, I'll be available when your leader and I are through."

As Keith talked, Nathan let his gaze stray to Stephanie, who was lying on a flat rock in a bit of shade. Small beads of sweat had formed on her brow, like sparkling diamonds. He liked her hair down. She seemed more approachable. Yes, she looked that way, but what had he just said about appearances?

six

Stephanie felt exhausted as she lay on the relative coolness of the rock. She hadn't slept well last night. Every natural sound of the desert sounded unnatural to her ears. Worry invaded her thoughts and then her dreams. These kids were as novice as she, and it troubled her to think their safety rested in her hands—hands she wasn't sure were capable of such a task.

Nathan seemed more than adept, but he acted like there were no risks involved. This caused her even more apprehension. On some level, it even irritated her that he had been sleeping soundly. True, his even breathing had been comforting, but that small concession didn't amount to much.

Earlier, when she awoke and saw him sitting nearby, quietly reading, the moment reminded her of the times late at night when she would find her father in the den, studying his Bible. The conscious comparison began to warm her, but then she balked, chastising herself for such thoughts. Soon thereafter she and Nathan had collided verbally again.

She remained quiet most of the morning as she observed his interaction with the group. Paula and Liz hung on his every word. Did they find him attractive? Could she blame them? His blue eyes could melt anything in their path. His muscular shoulders only emphasized the rest of his well-proportioned physique, which cast an impressive shadow. Ian and Keith were not so easily swayed but seemed to enjoy him just the same. She had been unable to read Heather or Tom's feelings since both were rather reserved.

Now, as she rested, she listened to his velvet smooth tones while he spoke quietly with Keith. Once again she felt comforted and the sensation scared her. Nathan caused a jumble of feelings, and she knew her emotional survival would depend on how far she could keep him away. She must constantly remind herself of the reason for this trip.

On some level she knew she admired Nathan. His spontaneity was enticing, even intoxicating. Eventually, however, as with most relationships, the thing that attracted her ultimately would become the thing she despised. In time, she would grow to resent this quality of Nathan's. So why not resist it in the first place? Besides, if she survived this little excursion, she'd never do it again. And this was where Nathan spent most of his life.

Stephanie sighed from the weight of her oppressing thoughts. Feeling weak and weary from the high heat of the day, she reached down to her pack to grab some lip balm. Her hand froze at the blow from a snake's strike. She hadn't been paying attention, despite all of Nathan's warnings.

Stephanie screamed and jumped back. Nathan appeared instantly at her side. His firm grasp on her kept her from tumbling off the rock in shock. She could feel his massive hands on her wrists and hear him talking to her as he lowered her to the ground, but for some reason she couldn't understand his words.

"What it is, Nathan?" Damian's voice reverberated in her ears.

Steph tried to answer. As she drifted in and out of awareness, she could hear panic in Paula's voice.

"Is she going to die?" No one seemed to be listening to the girl.

Kneeling at her side, Nathan turned her hand over and searched for something. "Steph, it looks like he got your watch strap. You're okay. I'm going to put some water on your face. Can you hear me?"

"If he didn't get her, why is she out?" Damian's voice asked.

"Probably the shock, fear, and heat. I've seen it before. She'll be fine. It's quite a scare for her."

He blotted her face with a wet bandana. She seemed aware of everything but couldn't will her body to move or her voice to speak. She felt suspended between heaven and earth.

The water Nathan drizzled over her soothed her, and her tense muscles began to relax. Finally, she opened her eyes.

"Don't try to sit up," Nathan cautioned, his hand resting on her shoulder.

Paula sobbed quietly nearby; Heather was silent.

"I'm fine," Stephanie said, more for herself than for the others.

"Let me see your wrist again."

Nathan turned her arm face up, pushed aside her watch-strap, and carefully examined the area. "Doesn't appear to have broken the skin, so I guess that heavy leather strap saved your life."

Stephanie nodded in agreement. "I was just reaching for my lip balm." Her voice trembled. "He didn't rattle. I saw him at the last minute."

"You probably startled him as much as he did you. And that's one thing I should mention. A rattler doesn't necessarily announce his presence before he strikes. That's a myth."

"Where do you think he went to?" Liz asked with trepidation.

"He's probably long gone. He's as afraid of you as you are of him," he said.

"I'm worried we're all going to die out here!" Paula had worked herself to near hysteria.

"What's our number-one rule?" Nathan asked her.

"Don't anticipate problems," she replied sheepishly.

"Exactly. I've never lost a party member yet." He winked at her and wrapped an arm briefly across her shoulders.

Stephanie watched as Paula smiled back warmly at Nathan. He had a wonderful way with her. As with most teenagers, everything was the extreme for this troubled girl, but he seemed to take it all in stride.

"Heather, maybe it's time for our special afternoon treat," he said.

"Right on it." She jumped up and pulled something out of her pack. "These are Hot Banana Boats," she said with pride as she lined each foil-wrapped package along the edge of the cook stove. "In a few minutes, everyone can take one."

"What's in 'em?" Ian asked.

"It's a surprise."

"You don't have to ask. It's obviously a banana," Keith chimed in.

The youth prattled back and forth until the treat was ready. Still feeling weak, Stephanie watched and listened. *Funny, I've learned more about these kids in two days than I have in two months.*

"Oooh, look. There's chocolate and marshmallows all melted in my cooked banana!" Paula squealed with delight.

"Who knew I couldn't live without a daily dose of chocolate?" Liz giggled.

My sentiments exactly, Stephanie thought as she devoured the delicious treat.

When everyone finished, they rested. There would be no hiking during the hottest part of the afternoon, and so each settled into what little shade they could find or make.

With her eyes closed, she eavesdropped on Nathan's conversation with Keith.

"If you watch what the animals do, you can learn a lot."

"I thought it was if you talk to the animals."

"See those quails? They head for water in the late afternoon."

"So the oasis is that way?" Keith pointed in the direction they were headed.

"Right."

"In the early morning and evening, the doves make their visit to the water."

"How'd you learn all this stuff, Uncle Nate?"

"I've made this journey many times. You learn more with each adventure."

"Even like the stuff you told us about drying wet matches by rubbing them through our hair?"

"That one I learned from a book and was glad I did."

His words faded as Stephanie drifted off to sleep, where her heart took control of her dreams.

❧

As they trudged along, Damian kept to himself, trying to hide his bad mood. The near miss with the snake, the unbearable heat, and annoying teenagers had taken a toll on him already. What he wouldn't give to be back in his air-conditioned apartment.

Stephanie was right about this camp not being suitable for her clients. He'd back her up when the time came. Of course, maybe he could help things along, as it were.

With every step he took, his head throbbed. He hoped his plans were worth this misery. His shoulders ached from the heavy pack. He wondered how she could carry one without complaining. In fact, when he looked around, he saw they were all loaded with a fair share. A rare feeling of contrition flooded to the surface, but only for a moment. After all, he wasn't used to this hard life.

His father, Alex Farrow, practically owned a corner of the world, and everyone did his bidding. Even Damian. Try as he might, he'd never been able to receive his father's approval, but all that was about to change. He could feel it. His luck was about to turn. Alex Farrow would marvel at what his son had done. How he wished it didn't have to mean the financial ruin of his father as well.

"You're awfully quiet, Mr. Farrow," Paula said sweetly.

"I'm enjoying the lack of pagers and cell phones," he lied. What could one possibly enjoy out here?

"Have you made this trip often?"

Damian glanced around to see who was within earshot. Too bad. Nathan was too close for him to answer in the affirmative. "I've taken many such courses. Just not desert ones."

"Which do you prefer?"

Go away, Kid, you're bothering me! Was proving himself to everyone so important that he'd have to put up with this twenty-questions routine? Yes. But he didn't have to like it. "I took a sailing course once. Three weeks of tough weather. I liked it best." He was getting good at making up stories as he went along.

"Yeah, I see you more as the water type. You don't look like you're enjoying the desert."

"That's where you're wrong, Paula. I am enjoying it." His words slipped out a little more harshly than he had intended.

"It's not easy, but I like it," he continued in a kinder tone.

Eventually, Paula grew tired of their conversation and trudged ahead in silence. Blessed silence for Damian.

The temperature cooled down while the pace seemed to pick up as the group moved along. He watched Stephanie talking with Keith. Now there was a pain in the neck if he ever saw one. No wonder his parents kept sending him away. A twinge of sadness threatened to crack his resolve. He'd been the rich kid sent away all his life.

He pulled out a stick of gum, threw the wrapper on the ground, and popped the piece into his mouth.

"Mr. Farrow!" Liz stopped, her arms akimbo. "Pick that up."

His face burned. He wanted to smack the mouthy kid. No one talked to him that way. He froze, resisting his initial response. She came and stood close to him. He straightened his spine and faced her square on, eye to eye. It irked him that she was so tall or that he was so—no, he wouldn't consider that. They warred silently, until finally he bent and picked up the litter. *Brat.*

Wait until I own this company, he boasted silently. As if that would make any difference. Once he owned this stupid company it would be shut down. The wonderful Mr. Moses and his useless parables would be out in the desert permanently. And it wasn't just Nathan who would lose.

He felt much better after that thought.

☙

Stephanie could smell the moisture in the air. The cottonwood trees stood like welcoming archways into the ethereal water palace that awaited them. Never before had she yearned for such a simple comfort.

Though Nathan had warned her the oasis would be small, she knew nothing could detract from the pleasure she would derive from being able to wash her hair. They worked quickly to get the fire going, find suitable places for each of them to sleep, and make dinner.

Stephanie was already tired of eating out of tinfoil, and this was only the second day. She missed using china and sterling silverware. She envisioned a crystal goblet with ice cubes floating in the purest water money could buy.

In the quiet of the evening, she stood, slipped a small packet of shampoo into her pocket, and headed in the direction of the oasis. Most of the group were in a heated discussion about the dwindling rainforest and didn't seem to notice she had left.

The camp was about two hundred yards from the water, and Stephanie approached the haven excitedly. She was surprised the liquid appeared so clear. Glancing around, she couldn't help but feel she'd been transplanted from the desert to some sort of exclusive health spa.

The dry, blistering ground had been replaced with yellow and green plant life. The stars glistened overhead, and a gentle breeze swayed the cottonwood trees. The winding waterbed pooled and flowed in an almost animated fashion as the hungry earth welcomed the refreshment. Just as she would, too. After taking off her shoes and socks and rolling up her pant legs, she stepped into the water. Disappointment washed over her. At least the tepid liquid was wet. Leaning forward and gathering all her hair, she lowered her head towards the trickling stream.

Without warning, someone grabbed her arm. "What do you think you're doing?"

Her heart thudded in her chest as the blood coursed through her veins. She whirled around with enough force to offset her attacker. At the last moment, she realized it was Nathan. "Don't ever scare me like that again! I nearly had a heart attack. I'm going to wash my hair, that's what." Fear had turned to anger, and she couldn't bridle her tongue.

"Get out of there now!" His voice scared her.

"Why? What's in there?" Her lips trembled as she jumped out.

"You can't bathe in there. How do you think we're going to fill up our water jugs? What do you think the animals drink? Didn't you hear me when I explained why we must camp so far from the oasis?"

Still trembling, she replied, "I wasn't thinking. I'm sorry."

Nathan nodded, and both of them glanced away from each other.

"You didn't have to scare me like that, you know."

"I'm sorry. I guess I got worried when I realized you weren't at the camp."

"Oh." *Calm down, Girl, it's not what you think. He's only worried about his reputation for never losing a party member.*

"I have a jug here. If you'd like, I'll fill it and help you wet your hair."

Her breath caught in her throat. Before she could answer, he scooped up some water. Then he pulled her over to a rock area and told her to·sit. He tipped her back until her hair hung over the edge.

Nathan carefully poured out the water, directing the flow to include the sides of her scalp. She could feel the heat from his body. When he leaned in to stop the water from escaping down her forehead, she felt his hot breath on her flushed face. Her pulse quickened at his nearness.

When her hair was sufficiently wet, he asked, "Where's your shampoo?"

Not daring to speak, she pulled the small package from her pocket and handed it to him. As he reached out, their hands touched.

Tenderly, in a circular motion, Nathan massaged her hair, creating a rich lather. When he lowered his face to scrub at the base of her neck, his two-day stubble brushed her temple. A shiver cascaded down her spine.

He piled her hair on top of her head and went to get more water. She watched from her peripheral vision as he reached deep into the stream bed. She couldn't miss how his shoulder muscles strained at the seams of his shirt. When he looked up after filling the jug, she turned her gaze to the sky. The stars twinkled with a brightness she'd never noticed before.

"Stunning, isn't it?" He tipped her head back farther and allowed her soapy curls to fall.

"It's so clear," she said almost breathlessly.

"Without the city lights for competition, the stars really

have a chance to shine, don't they?"

She tried to concentrate on his words but found herself thinking about his hands as he massaged her scalp. *Stop it!* she ordered herself. *This is the least he can do after frightening you so.*

"I feel like I could reach out and touch them," she murmured, very much aware that she'd rather reach out and touch Nathan.

"God's handiwork is truly amazing." He squeezed the excess water from her hair in a wringing motion that pulled on her head. "Feel better now?"

Stephanie pulled her head forward and turned to face him.

"Yes." The words sounded hoarse. He was so close she could hardly breathe.

Just when she thought her pulse couldn't race any faster, it did. Nathan leaned close, as if he were about to kiss her. She closed her eyes in welcome response.

"Here you are." Damian appeared almost out of thin air.

Stephanie jumped as Nathan backed away. *What perfect timing.*

"I'm glad I found you and not those kids," he snarled, tossing his head back in the direction he came from.

"I'm sure they wouldn't have been traumatized," Nathan said lightheartedly.

Damian grunted. "I don't think it's the kind of example you should be setting."

"I'm afraid I'm to blame," Stephanie said, trying to calm him. "I wanted to wash my hair and foolishly tried to do it in the water. Nathan caught me just in time. Shall we head back?" She left Nathan's side and marched past Damian toward the camp.

"Are you okay, Miss H.?" Keith yelled from the far side of the campfire.

She shivered. "Yes." The temperature had dropped rapidly. Or had it always been this cool, and she was too distracted to notice?

"You broke a rule, you know." He headed in her direction while the others watched.

"I did?"

Everyone laughed.

"You left without telling anyone."

So she had.

"Did Uncle Nate give you a lecture?"

No, something far better. "Did he tell you he would?"

"Nah. We just figured he would. You look cold. Join us by the fire."

"I think I will."

Soft music filled the night air as she and Keith sat down with the other teens.

"Ian, I didn't know you played the harmonica," she said.

Keith laughed. "He doesn't. That's an animal in pain somewhere nearby."

Ignoring Keith's comment, Steph listened quietly to a few bars of "Home on the Range." "This reminds me of when I was a kid. My mom would play the piano and we would sing." She looked around at the faces staring back at her. "Don't look so shocked. People did that kind of thing back in the good old days."

"Your mom carried a piano out into the desert?"

"No, Keith. I mean at home. Guess maybe it was a long time ago."

"You're not old," Liz said confidently.

"We used to love it. We'd sing in the car, in the backyard, wherever we went." She choked back tears. Never had she missed her family more than at this moment. Mesmerized by the glow of the flame, she was aware that Damian and Nathan were returning.

Ian continued to play his harmonica and Heather and Liz sang along. The girls' voices sounded so innocent and sweet.

When Nathan reached the fire, she studied his face. Was it her imagination or were his eyes smoldering?

❧

After another sleepless night, Stephanie saw things differently in the morning. While she had welcomed Nathan's tenderness the night before, she regretted accepting it so willingly now. This was not a social event and it angered her to think she had forgotten that. Damian finding them together only fueled her ire.

She should have been with the kids, not spending quiet time with their guide.

Take a deep breath, Steph. Who are you really mad at? Yourself, Damian, or Nathan? She shook off her frivolous thoughts and got up. She knew this was not the place for her clients, and soon Nathan would realize it, too.

Once again he was already up, reading quietly. Silently she slipped to his side. "Morning."

"Hi. How'd you sleep?" He seemed pleased to see her.

"Awful. I can't believe you like it out here."

"Though I love it out here, the desert takes on a whole new meaning when you share the experience with someone you care about." He reached for her hand, but she withdrew from him.

"Nathan, I'm not sure what happened between us last night, but I don't think it's wise for us to let our feelings get in the way of the job we're here to do."

His smile faded, and he slowly closed his book.

Had her words come out too harsh? What was she doing to this man? "My first priority is to those kids," she said, determined to stay focused.

"That's commendable. When do you take care of yourself?"

She looked away.

He reached for her hand again, and this time she didn't pull back. "You're running from something. What is it?"

"We're not discussing me." She stood and paced, her hands tightly jammed into her pockets.

"I'm sorry. Forgive me."

"I have serious doubts about the benefits of this trip."

"How can you say that? They are interacting very well. They're working as a team, helping each other with their designated duties. I've seen some growth already. Look at Heather. At first she played the weak female trying to get the guys to help. Now she willingly does things for herself. Haven't you noticed the change in her?"

"It's only a show and probably temporary."

"I don't think so. This camp is the type of thing those kids need. Some praise and attention for a job well done, support to grow as adults, guidance in decision making. It's the best thing they've ever done. I'm certain."

Damian's words drifted back to her. "He needs this to work out, or he'll lose his business." Studying the pain on his face, it suddenly became clear. It wasn't her he cared about; it was his livelihood. How could she have been such a fool? "I'm not so convinced."

She grabbed her water jug and headed for the oasis, being careful not to look back at Nathan. Tears stung her eyes. *Why am I crying?*

Seeing the rock she had sat on while Nathan washed her hair brought her emotions to the surface. She sat down and studied the amazing beauty surrounding her.

She heard Keith and Liz approaching and quickly wiped her eyes, hoping to erase all evidence of her tears. She watched as they laughed, stopped, and studied something on the ground, then continued toward her.

"Hey, Miss H., isn't it somethin' out here?" Keith said, dipping his jug into the oasis.

"Was it worth trekking twenty-five miles for?" she only half teased.

"You bet."

"Don't you think so?" Liz asked.

"I have mixed feelings at this point," she confessed.

Liz chuckled. "I was like that when I fell asleep last night. Boy, did I hurt!"

"Guess we should head back for breakfast and then hit the trail." Stephanie looked around. "If we can find it, that is."

When they returned, everyone was awake and getting ready for the day. Nathan seemed occupied with checking the assigned duties and ensuring each person understood what was expected of them.

"Heather, you look like you got too much sun. What are the signs of heat stroke?"

"I know, I know. I'm fine." She waved him away.

Moving to Liz, he said, "You were limping last night. How are you this morning?"

"Sore."

"Where?" He appeared so concerned for her well-being that Stephanie felt a hint of regret wash over her.

"My feet and my left shoulder."

"Let me look."

A rush of crimson colored the girl's face. "I—I—"

"If you don't mind," Stephanie said as she approached. She and Liz moved away from the others. Steph discovered deep bruising across the girl's shoulder. She touched the mark gently and Liz pulled away, wincing. Stephanie apologized for hurting her. "Let me see your pack."

Liz lifted it for her to examine. A sharp object protruded exactly where the pack met Liz's shoulder. No wonder the girl was in pain. "Hang on, Liz, I'll go talk to Nathan."

She walked back to the group and pulled him aside.

"What's up?" Though his words were casual, his attitude was anything but.

"Her shoulder is badly bruised. I told you those packs were too heavy." She spat out the words, wishing she'd never agreed to this.

Nathan put his hands on her shoulders. "I'm sorry, Steph. Let me finish checking with the gang, and we'll help Liz out."

"I don't think there is anything you can do to help. You know studies show that too much exertion is actually harmful. People benefit physically and psychologically from less strenuous workouts."

"And what study would that be? Your own?"

"No. There are several, and one of them happens to be from the University of Utah." *So there!*

Nathan sighed heavily, shaking his head. "Let me guess. You never colored outside the lines, did you?"

She caught the gleam in his eyes too late. "And what's that supposed to mean?"

"It means that you listen to too many studies. What about your experience? What does that show you? Anyone can misinterpret study results. And I can even produce a study from California that says wilderness excursions help people solve problems, think creatively, and manage stress better."

"Yes, well, that would most definitely be a misinterpretation." Her lips thinned in irritation.

"What I'm saying, Steph, is sometimes you've got to throw out the studies, the rules, and listen to your heart. Experience life and use that as your guide. We'll help Liz. Trust me," he said tenderly, then turned on his heel and walked away.

All she heard was him calling her Steph. He had spoken with such compassion she wondered how she could have doubted him. Of course, that didn't eradicate the fact that Liz was injured. Fighting a sense of despair, she readied herself for breaking camp.

Lost in her own thoughts, she didn't hear when Nathan ordered them to move out.

"Hey, Miss H., aren't ya coming?" Ian called.

Turning around, she burst out laughing. Each of them had painted their faces with colorful zinc oxide.

"We're waiting," Liz said. "Look what Uncle Nate did." She pointed to the practical use of his staff. Keith and Tom had the wooden stick braced between them with Liz's pack hanging from it.

Nathan turned back and hollered, "Time's a-wastin'."

Quickly, Stephanie shuffled into the center of the group and walked in unison with the others.

Well, he managed to solve that one easily enough. But what about the next problem? She forced the thought away.

seven

As they hiked across the dusty ground, Keith sang out like an army drill sergeant, "I don't know about my fate."

The other teens echoed his line.

"That's why we follow Uncle Nate."

They followed along laughing. Steph could tell Damian did not appreciate Keith's sense of humor. Secretly she enjoyed the fact they were annoying him so much.

Throughout the day, she watched Nathan, careful to avert her eyes when his gaze found hers. Her mind burned with the memory of his almost kiss. How she wished she could be some other place than out here with the one person who made her heart race—and her blood boil.

"Steph, you're limping."

Nathan's comment interrupted her thoughts. "I am?"

He helped her off with her pack and gently massaged her tired, achy shoulders. She rolled her neck until she spotted Damian watching them. "I'm all right now." She jumped away from him as if a scorpion had stung her.

"Let's look at your foot."

"It's fine."

"I'm going to find the little sage bush," Paula said suddenly.

"I'll join you." Stephanie needed a few minutes away from Nathan. In fact, she'd even welcome a large bird swooping down to carry her off right now.

"Nate's great, isn't he?" Paula said as they walked away from the group.

"Yes," she answered with little conviction in her words.

"He knows everything about the desert. And I can't believe how much I've learned. My teachers think I'm dumb, but Nate makes me believe I can do anything."

"It's wonderful you've gained so much confidence."

87

"Oh, it's more than that. He's changed my whole life."

"How so?" *Don't tell me you've fallen for Nathan!*

"Well, you know how I pretend to be the dumb blonde because everyone expects it? He told me to be myself and I'd be happier. Know what? He's right. Tom and I had a neat talk last night, and I think maybe he likes me."

Stephanie breathed an inner sigh of relief. Although Paula practically worshipped the ground Nathan walked on, she obviously recognized him as an authority figure and wasn't developing a crush on him. She hoped.

The last thing they needed on this trip was two women falling for Nathan Moses. *I can't believe I thought that!*

≈

"I think we should try this route," Ian said.

Nathan watched the teenager trace the map with his finger. This was their seventh day, and despite a few incidents all had gone well. The teens had risen to the challenge, surpassing any of his expectations. He had grown fond of each of them, and it seemed impossible to believe that in three more days it would all be over. "The decision is yours, Ian, but tell me the reason you want to go that way instead."

"We'll be traveling in the cool of the late afternoon and early evening. We'll be fresh from our siesta." He grinned. "It will cut our hike time down considerably, allowing us more time to rest at the oasis. Plus, it will really boost our confidence. I think we can do it."

"Okay, then. I'll let you tell the others after we've eaten."

Sitting down to his lunch, Nathan said a quick prayer. *Thank You, Lord, for this food and for the safety of those in my care.*

"Are we building the still today?" Tom asked.

Nathan nodded and swallowed his mouthful of food. "Yes. We'll get started after lunch."

Keith raised his hand as if in school. "Do we get another story, Uncle Nate?"

"I gather most of you think they're hokey." Nathan feigned hurt feelings.

A resounding no echoed throughout the camp.

"Okay, let me finish and then I'll tell you a short one. We've got lots to accomplish today, plus our leader has some important news." All eyes veered to Ian.

"It's not earth-shattering, guys."

Despite the interaction with everyone, Nathan's mind drifted back to Steph. Closing his eyes, he prayed. *Tell me how to reach her, Lord.* He'd beaten back his feelings for her as much as he could, but still they continued to grow, wild and fast like unwanted weeds. He pleaded with God to deliver him from temptation. Steph wasn't a Christian. They had no future together.

But the desire remained. His heart refused to listen to his logic. God needed to intervene, and fast.

When Nathan opened his eyes, he felt a physical pain in his chest as he watched Stephanie walk away from their circle with Damian. Before he could make a move to go after them, the kids entreated him for the story he had promised.

After only a few sentences about a man with a mule trapped at the bottom of a well, the interruptions began.

"And the farmer left his donkey stuck there?" Heather asked, her eyes wide and bright.

"Yep, he figured he could never get it out and assumed the fall had probably broken its legs."

"Oh, that's terrible," Liz said.

"Well, soon after, friends dropped by and told him he couldn't leave the mule like that. It was inhumane. The farmer agreed and decided his best course of action would be to fill in the well."

"How cruel!" Paula cried.

"It's not cruel," Tom corrected her. "Trying to pull the animal out could cause it more pain. Possibly break its neck and stuff."

"Oh, I don't like this story," she wailed, shaking her head.

"It gets better, Paula, trust me."

She waited.

"Now, with the first few shovelfuls, the mule starts braying with fright. Then the farmer hears nothing. Still, he continues to toss in the soil."

"If it's dead, why bother?" Paula played with the gold hoop through her ear while listening to Nathan.

"Well, you see, the mule panicked at first, but then a thought struck him. When a heavy load of dirt landed on his back, he would simply shake it off and move up. With every shovelful, the mule told himself, 'Shake it off and climb up. . . shake it off and climb up.' If panic began to overtake him, he'd keep right on shaking it off. After what seemed like an eternity, the battered and exhausted mule stepped over the wall of the well."

"Oh, thank goodness." Paula sighed with relief.

"And the moral is?" Nathan asked.

"You can't keep a good mule down?" Keith said with an air of innocence.

Nathan spit out his coffee with a guffaw. The rest of the group laughed with him.

"What? What's so funny?" Keith maintained his look of naiveté—all but the telltale twinkle in his eyes.

After Nathan regained his composure he finished the story. "What could have buried the farmer's livestock eventually helped him succeed. So when adversity seems to be falling all around you, use it to your advantage."

"Where do you get these stories?" Liz wanted to know.

"From the Internet," he replied, grinning at her. Then he turned to gaze longingly at Steph, who was still talking with Damian. *What is she doing with him?*

❧

"Now place the cut pieces of cactus on either side of the tin," Stephanie heard Nathan instruct as she and Damian drew closer to the group.

"Like this?" Liz asked as she followed his directions.

"Exactly. Now we grab that plastic sheet Tom has scratched up for us, and we cover everything like so." He carefully spread the plastic over the hole they had dug in the ground. "Then we seal it with the surrounding dirt and rock."

Paula stared at the items and wondered aloud. "How do we get water if it doesn't rain?"

"It's magic. You'll see." Nathan winked.

"What a fine-looking still," Stephanie said.

Damian nodded. "Makes me long for my pool."

"Think we could build one big enough to swim in?" Keith asked.

Nathan stood from his crouched position. "If you were the size of a fish."

The group laughed.

"You look awfully warm, Steph." Nathan's eyebrows furrowed as he gazed at her.

She resisted the concern in his voice and eyes. "I'm fine."

"Have you been drinking your full water requirements?"

She didn't want to tell him she hated drinking the warm water. Or that whatever fluid went in, twice as much seemed to come out. No matter how long they were out in the desert, she would never like visiting a sage bush. From now on, indoor plumbing would be her best friend. "Sort of," she hedged.

Nathan dug his fingers into the parched soil, pulled something up, then rubbed it on his pant leg. He handed the object to her. "Here, pop this into your mouth."

She backed away. "What is it?"

"It's a smooth stone."

"A rock?" She laughed. "You want me to put a rock in my mouth?"

"Yes. It will help saliva form and afford more fluid to your system."

Not taking her eyes off him, she reluctantly did as he said.

"Now get some balm on those dehydrated lips."

Steph felt like a little child being told what to do. Yet somehow she didn't mind. Squatting near her pack in the limited shade, she applied the soothing ointment. When she finished, she returned to the others.

"Ian is going to lead us through a different route tonight," Nathan began.

Stephanie's jaw opened, then snapped shut. She waited for him to continue, trying not to remember Damian's words.

"You can explain it, Ian, since it's your decision."

"Well, after studying the map, I thought if we went this way," he pointed so everyone could see, "climbing the mesa instead of going around, we'd get to the oasis faster tomorrow and have more time to rest."

"Nathan, have you ever gone this route?" Stephanie asked.

"I'm not in the decision-making process. It's up to them. Whether I've hiked it is not important."

"I think it is. They're only kids. You can't let them run their own lives."

"Hey, Miss H., we've been doing it for years. And we've been doing it since Uncle Nate brought us out here," Keith said.

"Yeah. He trusts us and our ability to think," added Paula.

"Well, you may think you've made all the decisions, but I'm sure—" Nathan jumped up and grabbed her hand before she could finish.

"Can I see you a minute, Miss Harris?"

As they walked away from the others, she wanted to give him a swift kick in the shins. How could he even think of letting them make a trek that might be unsafe?

"Do you remember back in the classroom I said I was always right?"

Did she ever! She folded her arms and glared at him. "How could I forget?"

"You seem to forget quite often." Now he crossed his arms and fixed his gaze on her.

"And what's that supposed to mean?"

"I can't even begin to count the number of times you have contradicted or questioned my leadership."

"I think you're mistaken. As the saying goes, you've had it your way from the start."

"I'm tired of arguing with you. You're the big psychologist who thinks she knows what's best for everyone. Well, I'm here to tell you that you don't even know what life is about. You're running scared and hiding behind that nice, cushy office you have, playing at being a nursemaid to those kids."

"How dare you—"

"I'm not done. I let you come along on this trip because I

believed you really did care about your clients, though you were perhaps a little misguided. I can see now I made a mistake. You have put your own fears onto them. They're not afraid to test their limits, to find out who they are."

"And you think I am?" She gulped for air.

"I didn't think so, but after what I've seen so far I'm beginning to think I misjudged you." His voice softened, and he kicked at the ground.

Steph clenched her fists and counted, waiting for him to continue.

"I don't mean to yell at you, Steph," he said, sounding contrite. "I think you have a heart of gold and everything you do is motivated by your concern for that strange group sitting over there, eyeing us closely. But they don't need someone to mollycoddle them. They need someone to respect them."

"I do respect them." She fought a tightness in her throat.

"Do you respect me?"

She swallowed hard. What *did* she think of him? "I'm not sure."

He sighed. "At least you're honest. I'll give you that."

"How big of you," she said, confused at how their explosive exchange had turned calm so fast.

"Well, where do we go from here? If you don't respect me, do you at least trust me?"

"Do you want my honest answer?"

Nathan burst into a hearty laugh. "I'm not sure. How 'bout we call it a truce for now? If you have any concerns, you can address them to me in private—not in front of them." He tossed his head back in the direction of the camp.

"We've sort of circumvented the whole reason we are over here having this little chat. I do have a problem. I have a problem with you letting them dictate where we hike tonight."

"As long as we don't anticipate problems or panic, I don't think there will be any trouble."

"You're mistaken if you think I'm panicking." Stephanie ached to resolve this merry-go-round with Nathan. It infuriated her every time they squared off, and a part of her just wanted to give in. Another part of her would never allow that to happen.

"I'm saying if we get into a situation out there, we'll be fine as long as we don't panic. Why do you take everything as a personal attack?"

"Is that what you think?"

"Why do you answer all my questions with another question?"

Before she could reply, he stepped forward, cupped her face in his hands, and stared at her in silence. She held her breath, willing her heart rate back to normal. He was too close. It unnerved her.

In an instant, Nathan released her and stepped back.

She gritted her teeth and clenched her fists. "What did you do that for?"

"Why do you think?"

"Because you like to play unfairly. You'll use my concern for those kids against me, and you'll use my feelings for you to your advantage."

"You have feelings for me?" The furrowed brow disappeared and seemed to be replaced by a flash of amusement.

"Yes. No. Oh, I don't know."

Nathan brushed a finger lightly down her cheek.

"Don't do that," she said, telling herself she didn't like his touches and private glances, but she knew better.

"Why?"

"Because."

He leaned closer. "That wasn't a good enough answer."

Steph arched away from him, worried about her reaction to his nearness. "Have you never heard of a little thing called personal space?"

He nodded and stepped even closer.

Steph fought the desire to let him encircle her in his arms and smother her with kisses. What was she thinking? She moved away from him again, as if they were in some sort of dance. How could she escape, knowing her heart had turned against her head?

"Hey, get a tent!" Keith yelled from the distance.

Without further words, they jolted apart from each other. Several feet separated them as they walked back.

Once again, Nathan had successfully sidetracked the real issue. In a few hours they would be headed out under Ian's direction down an unknown trail. Ignoring Damian's warning, Stephanie had let her heart decide, but at what cost?

Regret filled Nathan. What had he been thinking when he'd nearly kissed Stephanie again? That must be his problem, he decided—he hadn't been thinking. Normally he was pretty good at assessing situations and making the right decisions, but when it came to Steph, all common sense vanished.

He yearned for some time away from the rest of the group where he could cry out to God and get alone with his thoughts. He knew better than to become involved with a non-Christian, and especially someone who held his future in her hands. *Help me, Lord. I can't control these feelings.*

Nathan squeezed his eyes shut, willing himself to get some rest. In a little while they would be back on the trail. Sounds of a distant storm became a constant reminder to him of his relationship with Stephanie. One moment it would be quiet, and then suddenly the crashing thunder would gain everyone's attention.

He struggled to get control of his thoughts about the pretty blonde. In fact, he needed to stop dwelling on her and get his mind back on the job. Today's excursion could be crucial. He mentally checked off what needed to be done, then began a personal inventory of the group. Heather seemed withdrawn this morning. He'd have to keep a close watch on her.

He didn't know about Tom. He was still too quiet to assess. Ian's excitement about leading the group would benefit everyone. He hoped this enthusiasm wouldn't wane from the difficult climb ahead.

Paula was as confusing to him as Stephanie. At times she seemed not to have a clue, but then she would say something so intelligent he'd have to hide his shock. He believed she'd learned many things about herself already that would see her succeed at whatever she attempted.

And then there was Keith. While everyone enjoyed the light banter and funny comments, Nathan worried the teenager's frivolity was a wall. With such a blockade so firmly in place, Nathan knew it would take a lot to break through. He would remember to keep Keith—as well as all of them—in his prayers.

Nathan sighed. While everything seemed okay, he had a nagging feeling that something wasn't right. Had he stepped out of God's will? If that was the case, he knew disaster was never far behind.

eight

"Seems hotter today than yesterday," Stephanie said as she approached.

Nathan smiled, unable to hide his surprise and pleasure to see her step close to him willingly. Even if she should be resting like the others. The upcoming climb would be strenuous. "I'm worried you're not drinking enough fluids. Don't ration your water, Steph. You need it." As soon as the words were out of his mouth, Nathan regretted the way he'd ordered her to do as he said.

"I'll plop a rock in my mouth if I'm dry." She laughed.

"See, even you learned something out here."

She seated herself beside him. "Why do you love the desert so much?"

"I'm not sure," he replied, turning to look at her. "To me it is a wonderful world of miracles. Animals and plants adapt to survive in the extreme environment. It's amazing to see the life that flourishes in the dry, hard soil. Look around at the rock formations, the stark, blue sky."

"I must admit, some of it has been beautiful. When the sun set last night, the colors took my breath away. I know I've mentioned this lots, but I love the bright stars at night, too."

"That's my favorite. I think I feel closest to God then."

"I used to feel that way." Her words were barely audible.

"And now?" His gaze met hers briefly, and his heart ached when he saw the pain written across her desert-tanned face.

"I'm not sure. As a little girl, I would sit and look out my window for hours at the stars and moon and talk to God and wonder about the majesty of it all."

"What changed? The stars and the moon are still the same."

"But I'm not."

"Education can do that to you. Especially the sciences. How

can someone teach evolution yet believe in creation?"

"Oh, I lost my faith long before I got my degree."

He yearned to move closer and put his arms around her, but he kept his distance. *Help me, Lord!* "Care to tell me about it?"

She sighed and bit her lip. After looking away for a few seconds, she turned her face to him with a look of resolution. "My family had gone out on a hike. I rarely joined them on their all-day adventures, but I had wanted to go on this one."

He could tell she found it difficult to discuss this subject.

"Anyway, after they were gone I cried for awhile and then got interested in a book. I was so lost in my own little world that I never noticed how late it had become until a car pulled into the driveway." She paused and took a deep breath. "I assumed Mom and Dad and my sisters were finally home. Two police officers destroyed my world when they calmly told me my family—my whole family—had been killed."

"I'm so sorry, Steph." Taking both of her hands, he wrapped them securely inside his and studied the hurt in her eyes. "I had no idea. Now I understand why you don't want to be here. You're very brave. You know that?"

She shook her head. "I'm not brave at all, Nathan." The words came out in a whisper.

There appears to be more to her story, he thought. "So we're both orphans, dedicated to helping others. Somewhere deep inside you never lost your faith, Steph. You've transferred your Christian principles to your job and merely buried your connection to God. You know what's so wonderful? He's never left you. He's been inside your heart all this time. Exactly where you asked Him to be.

"It's like the dry riverbed we dug into yesterday to search for water. Remember how everyone was certain they wouldn't find anything? Then suddenly the water burst up the small hole. Dig into your heart, even a little bit, Steph, and God will come bursting through."

"I'm not so sure." A lone tear trickled down her cheek and splashed onto the back of his hand.

"You do know that God loves you no matter what, don't you?"

"I used to think that, but how can He after what I've done?"

Nathan chose his words with caution. "We've all sinned, but there's nothing you could have done that He couldn't forgive you for."

"I'm not so sure." She sighed. "Being out here has helped me see what a void I have in my life. Even this harsh land has more fruit than my own spirit."

He studied her slumped shoulders and the faraway look in her eyes. Nathan was certain it had been difficult for her to confess her feelings. He admired her strength. "You've been wandering around in the desert for a long time, Steph. Why not enter the Promised Land?"

She giggled.

"What's so funny?"

"I can picture what's next. Between your company, Burning Bush Adventures, your staff, your name—Moses—and all your parables and stuff, you'll be sending the plagues down on me if I don't obey you." She paused then added seriously, "Did God send you to lead me back?"

"If He did, I'm willing."

"I don't know if I am."

"You have to stop blaming yourself that you survived and your family didn't. You also have to let go of the bitterness over that loss. I know exactly how you feel. I lost my family, too, remember?"

"And you weren't angry with God?"

"Oh, I never said that." Now it was his turn to laugh.

"Hmm, do I hear another story coming on?"

"We don't have time for that. Want the condensed version?" She nodded.

"Sadly, I don't remember my parents at all. After a rough time in the group home, I ran away. When Mr. Moses found me, I hated the whole world and didn't even know about God. Mr. Moses fed me, clothed me, and offered support and love. It felt so good to me. After awhile, though, I only saw the things I didn't have."

Nathan slipped off the rocks and paced as he talked. "Whenever we would go to church, I'd sit there and tell God how unfair my life was. Everyone in the room had family, nice cars, and houses. I had nothing. I became angry and lashed out many times. But Mr. Moses remained patient."

"Sounds like you were very lucky to have him."

"But I didn't know that. One day, while out hiking, I ran off without thinking and got lost. It turned cold, and I wasn't prepared. As I shivered under a bush, believing I would die that night, I made my peace with God.

"I poured out all my pain and anger and then sat very still. After a few moments, I added a postscript to my prayer. I said, 'If you love me, God, send someone to save me.' I'm sure that it was just the wind howling that night, but I heard the word 'Jesus.'

"I didn't think too much about it at first because a few minutes later Mr. Moses found me—again. But later, at home in my own bed, as I drifted off to sleep, I remembered the sermons from church and realized God had already sent someone to save me. Jesus. A shiver ran down my spine that night. I did nothing to rid myself of my bitterness and anger. I gave it to God and He took care of it."

Steph looked away. "You make it sound so easy."

"It's not easy. Sometimes you have to keep giving it back to God. But it's that simple."

"I've prayed and asked God to show me things, but I've never really felt He's heard me."

"Perhaps you were looking in the wrong place for the answer. At first, it seemed that Mr. Moses was the answer to my prayer. Only later did I realize he wasn't—Jesus was."

"I admire you, Nate. Your faith is so much a part of you. But I feel uncomfortable talking about God—even praying."

"That's normal when you're not used to it. Let me ask you this. Did you feel comfortable the first time you drove a car?"

She shook her head.

"Of course not. But after doing it for awhile, you did. And now driving a car is as natural for you as breathing, isn't it?"

"Of course."

"Yet, when you think about it, for sixteen years or more you never drove, then suddenly you could. Now you may have only been driving for ten years, but I bet you can hardly remember not ever driving."

"You make a valid point. If not long-winded."

"It's my gift," he said, and they laughed together.

"You know, my parents raised me in a church. I should be more comfortable talking to God." She sighed. "So why don't I?"

"Poke your finger into the ground right there." She eyed him carefully and then jumped down from the rock and did as he said.

"It won't go in. The ground is too hard."

"That's what your heart is like, Steph. You've hardened it to Him. You've allowed your pain to build up scar tissue so deep it's rock solid."

He watched her brush the dust from her hands. His heart swelled with emotion. *Help me help her, Lord.*

"I see," she replied with a shaky voice.

"I'm not saying this to hurt you." *Because I'm sure I've hurt you enough.*

"Oh, I know," she said quietly.

"I've come to care for you, Steph. I'd like to see you get right with Jesus."

"Is that the extent of your concern? Leading me back to the Lord?"

He winked at her. "Oh, nowhere near the extent."

She playfully tossed a small pebble at him. "Do I trust you?"

"Always." He couldn't resist grinning.

"I'll think about what you've said, Nate. Or should I say Moses?" she bantered. "I guess I have some stuff to work out first."

"I'd like to say 'do it for me,' but do it for yourself. No matter how things turn out on this trip, you deserve to receive all of God's blessings. You're very special." When she flashed a half-smile at him, he could tell he had embarrassed her with his comments. And she had rejected them like the hard ground beneath them. He could see the wariness in her eyes. How he longed to hold her and keep her safe.

"That's very sweet of you to say."

Silence fell for a few minutes. "Well, I guess our afternoon rest time is almost over. We should get ready to head out," he said.

She nodded and turned away.

≈

Nathan's right, she thought a short time later as she hiked along with the group. She'd allowed her pain to cloud her vision. Hurt had invaded her very being and taken root in the form of anger and bitterness. But could she give all that over to God?

A part of her resisted. Her culpability. She hadn't told Nathan the whole story. He wouldn't want anything to do with her if he knew the truth. God already knew, and He'd distanced Himself from her a long time ago.

Why then did she feel drawn to God? Was it because of her growing feelings for Nathan? Or could she be reaching out because of a deep need to come face-to-face with her past? To admit that what she'd done had been wrong?

Whatever the reason, she had plenty of time to dwell on it while they hiked toward the mesa.

Every once in awhile, the distant drum-roll of thunder spooked her, and as the sun began to drop from the sky, she thought she could see an occasional flash of lightning.

The gang was merrily marching along, laughing, joking, singing, and keeping an eye on the storm-show being played out against the sky. She appreciated their resilience and suddenly felt a crush of failure in her own life. She had been existing as a shell. Cut off from those important to her. Oh, sure, she cared about the kids, but that wasn't good enough for them or for her.

"A D.S. for your thoughts," Keith said, stopping for her to catch up to him.

"I'm admiring the sky—from afar!"

"Here you go," he said, handing her something.

Instinctively, she held out her hand to receive it. "What's this?" Before Keith could reply, she screamed and dropped the small furry thing he had placed in her palm. Everyone stopped and stared at her.

"Oh, Miss H., you've hurt him," Keith groaned as he bent to survey the wounded animal.

"I'm sorry, but what did you do that for?" She watched him cradle the tiny gray creature tenderly.

"I told you I'd give you a D.S. for your thoughts. You told me your thoughts, and so I followed through with the goods."

"What on earth is a D.S.?"

"The cutest little thing you ever saw. Look at him. He's a desert shrew."

Stephanie resisted the urge to say something awful. Rodents, in her book, were not the type of creatures you cuddled. "I'm sorry, Keith."

"He seems okay now. Probably a little deaf from your wake-the-dead shriek and stunned from skydiving without a parachute."

She forced herself to look at the shrew resting in his palm. It had pink inner ears, a long thin tail, and tiny feet. The little fellow wasn't more than three or four inches long, nose to tail, and fit perfectly in his hand. "Where did you find him?"

"Back where we rested."

"Isn't there a law that we can't take anything with us?"

"Yeah, Keith. You were supposed to leave him where you found him," Paula said. "He scared me with the little thing, too, Miss H."

Keith smiled. "Sorry, I didn't know we had females afraid of a *little thing* like this in our group."

"I think you should let him go. We haven't traveled that far," Stephanie said.

He looked back. "Well, maybe for us it hasn't been too far, but I think for him it will probably take his whole lifetime to get back."

Stephanie looked at Nathan, who had not said anything

yet. In fact, everyone seemed to be watching them. "What do you think, Nate?" she asked.

"It's up to Keith," he replied.

Damian mumbled something indiscernible.

Lord, help me, she thought, then realized it had been years since she let those words cross her mind. In this moment, they had come so easily, almost naturally.

"Miss H., don't move," whispered Heather.

She froze, fearful that another snake stood poised to strike.

"Ah, it's only a common butterfly," Damian said with a sneer.

"So, it's pretty," argued Liz.

From the corner of her eye, Steph caught sight of the lemon-yellow and black insect where it rested on her shoulder.

"We need to keep moving, gang. We haven't got all day," Ian said, motioning for everyone to follow him. The butterfly flew away, and Keith gently placed the shrew beneath a bunch of desert agaves.

They moved on in silence. Ahead of them loomed the massive mesa they would soon be climbing. Her heart skipped a beat whenever she looked at it. She recognized the same fear she felt when looking at Nathan. They both represented the unknown to her. Could she climb the mountain? Could she let herself fall in love?

She pulled a moist towelette from her pocket and wiped her face.

Keith fell into step with her. "Hey, I'm real sorry about the shrew."

"No problem. He was kind of cute."

"I never thought I would be hurting him. Think Uncle Nate is ticked off with me?"

"Doesn't sound like it. If you're worried, ask him." She smiled at him reassuringly.

"Nah. I'm not worried."

"What about the climb?"

"Nothing to it." He sounded very confident.

"I hope we get a good meal after."

"Hey, I'm a great cook!" he exclaimed in mock offense.

"I warn you, I'll be starved after the workout. And I probably won't be the only one."

"Seriously, Miss H., it's not a bad climb. Uncle Nate says we can even eat dinner at the top. He said it's an awesome view to wake up to. Too bad we won't be camping out on it."

"That is too bad. I imagine it will take me a whole night to recover."

"It ain't so tough. You gotta stop worrying 'bout everything. We're having a blast. 'Cept for old Stuffed Shirt there," he said as he nodded in Damian's direction. "I don't trust him."

Stephanie stifled a laugh. "Is there a reason, or just your gut instinct?" She tried to keep the tone of her voice light.

"Mostly my gut. He sure harps on about everything. And he doesn't seem to know much."

Hmm, guess I was right about Damien. "Maybe he doesn't like being around kids."

Keith lowered his voice, which wasn't necessary since they were now quite far behind the group. "He has things in his shoes to make him taller. Ain't that dorky?"

"No worse than wearing a leather jacket to look tough, I suppose." She smiled, knowing that until this trek she'd never seen Keith without his leather coat.

"Aw, that ain't cricket, Miss H."

They both laughed.

"Hey, slowpokes. What's your problem? Can't walk and talk at the same time?" Ian hollered back to them.

"Put a sock in it, why don't ya!" Keith quipped.

"Well, quit your jabbering and catch up."

They scurried ahead to join the group. "Are you satisfied?" Keith asked.

"Now, children," Liz interrupted, and both Ian and Keith glared at her. "What? I'm only joking."

Stephanie shivered as she watched the interaction.

"You okay?" Nathan asked as he approached her, gravel crunching under his heavy boots.

"What I wouldn't give for a nice, long, hot bath," she confessed.

"Is that all? I could use a decent cup of coffee."

"Sshh, you'll hurt the cook's feelings."

"Right," he whispered. "If we make him angry, we'll be eating baked shrew for dinner." He grinned, and the smile extended to his beautiful blue eyes, where it seemed to linger and sparkle.

"Please don't remind me of that incident."

"Good thing he wasn't hurt the way you tossed him down." His smile seemed permanently pasted on his face. She knew he was having some fun with her.

"Keith surprised me, that's all."

"A *little thing* like that?"

She spun around to glare at him but saw the gleam in his eyes.

"What? No reply? Shrew got your tongue?"

Steph merely smiled.

nine

This is no place for any human. Miss Harris better realize that and act accordingly. It's good she's afraid to climb the mesa. I can use her fear to my advantage. Sorry, Uncle Nate. Damian resisted the desire to laugh out loud.

Under other circumstances this trek might have been fun, but he needed to see Burning Bush Adventures shut down. Business took precedence over everything.

Finally, he would outdo his father. He would no longer be thought of as the loser in the family. They'd look up to him. They'd see they had underestimated him. And then they'd hate him. Still, he would have gotten their attention. Hadn't Stephanie said something about bad attention being better than no attention at all? Was he just like the kids she dealt with? No, this was different.

He'd worked hard for many years trying to please his father. Or anyone in his family. But no one ever paid him any mind. This, they would notice. And in reality it had been rather easy. A little backstabbing here and there, a few underhanded real estate deals, a couple of untruths, and everything was falling into place.

Even here in the desert, all he'd done was say, "There, there, you're right—this is a nasty place" a few times and plant a few seeds of doubt and dishonor. Yes, it had all been so easy.

He repositioned himself beside Stephanie. "It's going to be a beautiful night, despite the distant storm."

"How can you tell?"

"There's no moisture in the air." He looked skyward as he spoke.

"Damian!" Stephanie cried as he stepped in front of her. She tried to remain upright after tripping over his foot, but the heavy pack on her back threw her off balance. Her ankle

107

twisted as she landed awkwardly on the hard ground.

"Sorry," Damian said weakly as he tried to help her up.

She groaned in pain while rubbing her foot.

"Let me look at it," Nathan said when he reached her side. Holding her heel carefully in his hands, he rotated her ankle slightly while watching her face.

Ah, yes, the hero has to get in here. I could have helped her up.

"She looks okay to me."

"I don't think she is. Look at how pale she's become."

"I'm okay. Give me a minute."

Glancing up, Damian noticed the group had continued to move ahead, although slowly. "Shouldn't you be dealing with those kids?" he asked Nathan.

"They know what they're doing."

What can I do now to get rid of him? This is my only chance to convince Stephanie to turn back.

❧

"Really, I'm okay." Stephanie tried to stand.

"I don't think so." Nathan helped her maintain her balance. She forced herself to ignore his strong hands supporting her.

She winced in pain. "Let me walk a little on it."

"Hang on, I'll put a tight bandage on it first." He helped lower her back down to the ground.

Steph closed her eyes as Nathan wrapped her injured ankle. When he finished, she glanced up at him and noticed the sky had darkened considerably. She shivered.

Paula's sudden scream echoed in the stillness.

Nathan released Steph's ankle, and she winced as her foot landed with a dull thud. She ignored the pain and watched as Nathan raced to the group. She managed to stand, despite her injury, and her mouth fell open in shock. "What on earth?"

Damian moved to her side and took her arm. "We need to get out of here! It's a flash flood."

Fear coursed through her veins. "Grab Nathan's pack! We've got to help." She limped forward, ignoring the pain. Damian followed. Her gaze remained transfixed on the frightening scene ahead while they made their way to what appeared to be a once-dry riverbed or gully.

Steph watched Nathan tie a rope around his waist. "Don't!" she shouted at him, but he didn't hear her over the rushing water and Paula's intermittent screams.

He had already entered the raging water to rescue Paula while everyone else grabbed onto the rope. Damian appeared hesitant but then took hold as well.

Stephanie cried out in anguish as she neared the raging waters. Where was Nathan?

Paula had managed to grab hold of a rock overhang, but the forceful current continued to rise. The girl hung precariously to the edge, her arms and screams obviously weakening. Steph took hold of the rope with the others as they scrambled to maintain their balance.

Nathan had disappeared under the rush of water. Silently, Steph began counting. One. Two. Three. Four. Five. Would he make it back up? Six. Seven. Eight. *Lord, please save him.* Nine. Ten.

Suddenly, he bobbed to the surface closer to Paula, and everyone breathed a sigh of relief.

"Oh, no!" Liz cried out when Nathan disappeared again.

Glancing around, Stephanie realized the water was dangerously close to flooding the entire area. If it got much higher, she knew Nathan and Paula would be unable to survive. They would all be at risk in a matter of minutes. Could she let go of the rope? Could she sacrifice two for the sake of the others?

Steph visually searched the area. Water poured down the gully alongside the mesa like a torrential rain, filling the culvert to almost overflowing. If the flooding continued it would soon spread to the ground they now stood on. No one would escape.

She studied the mesa they had planned on climbing and spotted a ledge about eight feet off the ground.

Lord, please hold back the water until we can get out of the way. While the others held tight to the rope and Damian shouted instructions, Stephanie grabbed two of the packs. Still limping, she made her way to beneath the overhang. Spinning around like a wind-up toy, she released the first pack. It sailed through the air to the ledge. She threw the second one the same way. It fell short. Hurriedly, she tried again and was successful.

She raced back and grabbed onto the rope just as Nathan got to Paula.

"Yes!" several voices shouted in unison.

Was it possible they would all be safe?

"Pull!" Ian shouted from the front of the line, his voice raised in a fearful pitch.

"I can't," Heather sobbed.

Keith turned to her. "Yes, you can. They're almost here."

Steph scanned the area. A feeling of dread swept over her, but she refused to give up. She pulled back with all her strength.

"We're all going to die!" Heather wailed.

"Don't think about that. Think about pulling. Close your eyes and imagine yourself pulling them out," shouted Tom.

"I can't."

"Do it!" Ian ordered.

Heather cried even harder.

"Hang on a little longer, Heather," Stephanie said, hoping to hide her own fear. "They're almost close enough to haul out."

Silence hung in the air as everyone concentrated. Steph pulled and stepped back. She pulled again. Were they winning this fight against nature?

"Hold tight. I'm gonna let go to help Paula." Ian moved closer to the edge of the gully while Damian surged forward.

Stephanie could feel the line begin to drag her toward the edge of the gully. She fought against the pull, but her hands were weakening and her foot ached.

As Nathan pushed Paula up out of the raging river, Ian grabbed her limp arms and dragged her over the edge. She collapsed in exhaustion, but no one dared let go of the rope until Nathan had been rescued, too.

"I'll be there in a minute, Paula," Stephanie called to her. "As soon as Nathan's out. We're going to be fine." *Please don't make me a liar, Lord.*

Nathan suddenly vanished under the water. The pull on the rope from the raging river appeared too forceful to argue with.

"Where is he?" Liz's voice quivered.

"Keep holding," Tom answered. "Pull hard."

Stephanie began counting again. *Oh, no, Lord, please.* Without warning, Ian jumped into the water.

"NO!" Steph shouted in a panic. "No. Oh, no." *God, help us! Please don't let Ian get swept away.*

A surge of water crested over the edge of the bank. Stephanie let go of the rope and raced to where she'd seen Ian go in.

The world stood still, save the raging water. Should she resign herself to the loss? Should they let go and care for Paula? Was this the way it would end? She blinked back tears. She'd been a fool. She'd said things she hadn't really meant. *Give me another chance, please, Lord.*

In an instant, Ian bobbed to the surface not far from the edge. "He's unconscious," he shouted breathlessly, dragging Nathan's limp body with him.

Damian strained as he held the front of the rope. Steph took hold as well. She studied each person on the line. They were weary. Would they have the strength to pull Ian and Nathan to safety?

"We can manage," Tom said as Paula stepped forward to help.

"He saved me," she said in a husky whisper. "I owe him."

No one responded.

Ian helped push Nathan up while Damian leaned down to grab Nathan under his arms and drag him from the edge. Next Damian helped Ian.

The guys carried Nathan toward the base of the mesa.

"Grab the packs. There's a ledge up there," Steph said as she pointed. "We need to keep everything dry." She longed to stop and make sure Paula was okay, but it would have to wait.

The water continued to rampage down the course of the riverbed, but the worst of the flood had been maintained within its banks. Stephanie's breathing slowed as she surveyed her surroundings.

Hugging Heather when she reached the ledge, she said, "You did fine out there."

"I'm sorry, Miss Harris. I was scared."

"You weren't the only one."

Tom came over to Heather and gave her an embarrassed hug. "You were great, Kid. Have a little faith in yourself. There's no way we could have pulled them out without you."

Heather's face lit up from Tom's gracious comments. "Really?"

"Really." He gave her chin a gentle chuck.

Steph could have hugged Tom, but loud voices took away from the moment.

"I don't think so," she heard Ian say.

"I'm telling you he needs CPR." Damian's face reddened and his neck muscles strained as he spoke.

Ian remained calm. "Nathan said only if a person wasn't breathing. He's breathing fine, but we can't leave him on his back. If he vomits, he'll die."

Steph hobbled over. "Damian, I think Ian is right. I remember Nathan saying something about the rescue position. On his side, with his leg bent up and over in front."

"Right, Miss H."

Damian shrugged. "Whatever."

"We need to be careful of his neck when we move him," Tom added. "And keep him warm."

Gently Ian and Tom shifted Nathan, bending his knee to ensure he didn't roll over.

Stephanie reached for Nathan's pack and nodded to Ian and Damian. "Can you get him out of those wet clothes?" She turned to Paula. "You need to get into something dry, too."

Liz brought Paula her backpack. "Here, I'll hold up your sleeping bag. You can change behind it."

With chattering teeth and trembling hands, Paula did as Liz said.

While Nathan was changed, Stephanie turned away and

tried to think of a way out of this mess. "Damian, do you have a radio we can use?"

He didn't answer.

"Damian!" she called. When he answered, she asked him again if there was a radio.

"I don't think so."

"How do we get out of here?"

Silence.

She turned to look at him. Nathan was now in dry clothes, and Damian seemed to be studying the raging water as it continued its journey toward an unknown destination. "Damian! How do we get out of here?"

He shrugged.

Steph resisted the urge to scream at him.

"Nathan showed us a mirror he has with a hole in the middle for signaling for help," Keith said.

"He told us anything shiny will do. We've got tinfoil here." Liz patted one of the packs. "Oh, and Ian's sunglasses!"

Though her panic had lessened, Stephanie worried their troubles had only just begun. With Nathan still out cold, no radio, no sun to signal for help, and no one knowing what to do next, all the necessary elements were in place for a disaster. If this wasn't already one.

Checking on each member of the group, she saw no serious injuries had been sustained. Paula had several cuts to her face and hands, which Liz had already bandaged, while Heather had provided some ointment for their blistered palms.

As Ian changed behind a sleeping bag, they made jokes to help ease the tension from the incident. *What a terrific bunch*, Stephanie thought.

When Paula settled on the ground, Stephanie sat beside her. "What happened?"

"I've never been so scared in all my life. I noticed a small trickle of water in the bottom of the ditch or creek bed or whatever that thing is there." She pointed to where she had stood. "While the others were chattering over which one of the guys would win your heart, I thought I'd wet my sore, tired feet. So I took off my shoes and socks and scooted down the side into the center of it.

"I never really noticed that the trickle wasn't still a trickle until suddenly I heard this strange noise." She shivered. "It sounded like a wild bear roaring behind me. I think maybe I froze for a moment, then I turned. All of a sudden this huge wave smashed into me, and I went flying. I can't believe the force of that thing nor how much water I swallowed.

"If I hadn't been able to shove myself up from the bottom and grab that overhang there, I'm certain I would have drowned. I nearly let go several times. It felt like my arms were being ripped from my shoulders."

"Are they okay now?"

"Both are pretty sore, but I think my head hurts more than the rest of me."

"Are you warm enough?"

She nodded. "Liz said my lips were blue. Are they still?"

"A nice healthy pink now." She patted Paula's shoulder.

"Oooow."

"Sorry. You really are tender. Try resting for a bit."

If it were in her power, Steph would call someone to pick them up. But, for the first time, she wondered what that would do to each of them. They'd worked hard to pull Nathan and Paula back to safety, all thanks to Ian's quick thinking and leading. As Ian huddled at the base of the rock formation, Steph walked over to him. "Are you okay?"

He nodded.

"What do you think we should do? Try to find help, or wait here until Nathan comes around?"

"I've been thinking about this. Maybe everyone should climb the mesa anyway, while I wait here with him."

"Do you think it's wise to separate?"

"Yeah, you're right. I heard somewhere that everyone should stay together." He scraped a stick in the rocky soil as if contemplating something. "I guess maybe we should have a meeting and discuss our choices."

"Good idea."

They joined the others.

"Okay, Miss H. and me were discussing what we should do, and we're gonna take a vote."

"A vote for what?" Damian asked.

"I dunno yet. First we gotta decide what to do."

"We can't do anything till he wakes up," Keith said, pointing to Nathan.

"And what if he doesn't wake up for days?" Paula asked with a quiver in her voice.

"Well, I've been sitting here thinking," Tom started slowly. "My jean jacket here is the same as Ian's. A lot of thick branches are floating over there. Can we get two long ones, cut off the pieces, then slip the arms of our jackets over them and snap them together to form some sort of a stretcher?"

"We could maybe use some of the rope and tie him to it, and then drag it so it's not too heavy," Stephanie added.

"Sounds good," Ian said. "But the next question is, drag it where? Do we all wait here while some of you go for help? Or do we try and get to the pick-up site?"

"I think it's best if we leave two of you here and the rest of us go on," Damian said.

Heather nodded her head in agreement.

"As much as I'd like to go on, we don't know how injured he is," Tom spoke with hesitation. "Maybe we should wait out the night. If he doesn't come to by morning, we should try and signal for help."

"What if another flash flood hits?" Heather asked, her voice trembling. "This time it might flow over the banks, and we all could be trapped."

"I think we're safe," Ian said calmly. "Although it's still rushing past us, I can see it's lower."

"I'm in favor of waiting out the night to see if Uncle Nate is awake by morning," Liz said.

"Me, too," joined Keith.

"Me, three," added Paula.

"I'm not," Damian said with a forceful tone. "I think someone should go for help."

"What? You can't be serious." Ian stood and spun around to face Damian. "It's not safe to split up. Or were you thinking of going alone?"

"Yes, if I have to."

Steph was surprised by Damian's comment. "I don't think that's a good idea."

Ian nodded in agreement. "So, all those who say we wait until morning to decide what to do, raise your hand." Everyone except Damian voted in favor of Ian's suggestion. "Do we make camp here?"

"Can anyone climb and see how wide that ledge is up there where I threw two of the backpacks?" Stephanie asked, pointing to them.

"When did you do that?" asked Keith.

"When it looked like the water would flood this area. I could only carry two—"

"I'll climb up there," Ian interrupted.

While the guys helped Ian, Stephanie finally had a moment to examine her tender foot. Though puffy and sore, there was minimal bruising. *Hopefully, it's not broken.*

Next she looked through Nathan's pack. In an outer pocket, she discovered a small hand-held radio. "Damian," she called as she jumped up and headed toward the group. "How do we call for help?"

"Turn it on first," Tom suggested.

"That would help, wouldn't it?" Steph said. When nothing happened, she handed the radio to Damian.

"Guess it's dead," he said after a few minutes of trying to get some sort of response.

Steph kept her disappointment to herself. "On to plan B, then."

"Hey, Miss H.," Ian said, interrupting their conversation. "It's wide enough for us to sleep up here."

"Really?" *Finally, something good.* She glanced around at the weary group and then eyed the water level. Getting to higher ground would be a good move.

"But how do we get Nathan up here?"

A good question. Maybe all the kids could stay up on the ledge while she and Damian slept down below with Nathan. But how would that look? Plus, she didn't like the idea of the girls up there with the guys. Especially since Heather seemed so vulnerable right now. It was either everyone up or everyone down. And everyone down might mean a soggy night if the water rose.

"Guess we'll pull him up the same way we pulled him from the water," Keith said, holding up the rope. "This will be like one of those stupid math puzzles we had to do in school. You know, you got a boat with three people on shore, and you can only go across twice, but your boat only seats two, yadda, yadda. . ." His voice trailed off.

Liz jumped to her feet. "It's simple. Ian stays up there and helps Paula, Heather, and me climb the rope to the top with you and Tom holding it tight down here. Then you tie Nathan to the rope and we help Ian pull him up—"

"I think we need another guy on the ledge before we pull up Uncle Nate," Tom said.

"Okay, whatever. But it can be done," Liz finished.

"One other thing." Stephanie held up her hand to stop them all from scrambling to the ledge. "Can we have a fire up there to keep Nathan and Paula warm so they don't catch pneumonia?"

Ian looked around, then shouted back. "I wouldn't risk it."

"I'm warm now, Miss H.," Paula said with a shiver.

Stephanie laughed. "Are you sure?"

"Yep."

Kneeling down to feel Nathan's forehead, then his hands, Stephanie decided that he seemed warm also. *Good*, she thought. *Oh, not good. What if he has a fever now?* "Okay, let's get up on that ledge."

The packs were lifted first, then the girls. With great care they hoisted their comatose guide. Despite a few bumps along the way, he reached the meager summit. Everyone cheered. Once positioned, little room remained to move, and they passed a cold dinner to one another like a bucket brigade during a fire.

As the night grew still and the water calmer, Nathan became restless. He thrashed about, all the while mumbling. Though no one else in the group could understand what he murmured, Stephanie thought she knew what was on his mind. Several times he'd uttered her name.

She sat beside him, keeping a close watch, and when sweat would bead upon his brow, she would tenderly wipe it with one of her lemon-scented wipes. A few times, when he seemed to be tossing about the most, she tried to wake him gently, but he remained unconscious. Tom assured her that as long as Nathan remained in the rescue position, he would be fine. But she had her doubts.

As the others drifted off into quiet sleep, Stephanie remained close to Nathan. She, too, felt tired. In fact, once her adrenaline had subsided from the flood, weariness threatened to overcome her. She forced her eyes to stay open.

As she fought sleep, she remembered a story in Luke about a rich man with a beautiful purple robe. Closing her eyes briefly, she could easily envision the beggar, Lazarus, covered in sores, as he sat outside the rich man's gate. As the story played out in her mind, a verse came to her about the man asking Lazarus to dip his finger in water and cool his tongue.

That's it! Grabbing her water bottle, she poured some water on her fingertips and slipped them into Nathan's mouth. She repeated the act several times.

Throughout the night, whenever Nathan became agitated she gave him water until he seemed calmer. She wiped his forehead with a gentle touch. She rummaged through her pack and pulled out some dried apple slices, raisins, and nuts. The food kept her awake and satisfied the grumbling in her stomach.

While eating, she tried to remember some other Bible verses. One from Jeremiah popped into her thoughts. *"I will refresh the weary and satisfy the faint."*

Eventually, the sun began to rise. They had survived the night. It was one of the most grueling incidents of her life. Not unlike the first night after the loss of her family. Tears filled her eyes. She rarely allowed herself to think about that time. A rush of emotion inundated her, and she bit back the tears. *Thank You, God, for giving me loving parents. People who made me learn my memory verses every week!*

Steph marveled at how easily she had prayed. Could Nathan have been right? Was God waiting patiently for her, and all she had to do was call upon Him? She took a vast amount of comfort in that thought.

Finally, when the sweat ceased from Nathan's brow and he seemed to thirst no more, Stephanie remembered one last verse, which caused her to smile. "*Strengthen me with raisins, refresh me with apples, for I am faint with love.*"

🏵

Nathan stirred, opened his eyes, and tried to sit up but couldn't. His head throbbed and his arm felt weighted down. Everything seemed blurred as he strained to recognize his surroundings. After blinking several times he could make out images, but where was he?

His chest hurt whenever he breathed. A dull ache stretched across his lower back, and his knees twinged occasionally. His right arm felt numb and tingly. He didn't need a medical degree to figure out why his arm troubled him. A woman's head rested on it. The sweet innocence on her face seemed almost angelic.

Small wisps of blonde hair danced about her temple in the breeze. Her breathing sounded rhythmic—and heavy. Just like her head on his arm.

When he tried to move, she woke up and stared at him. Embarrassment flushed her cheeks. "I'm sorry, I guess I fell asleep—oh, you're awake!"

"Ssshhh," he replied, reaching for his head.

"I'm sorry," she whispered. "How do you feel?"

"Like I've been run over by a Ram."

She looked confused. "As in a big sheep?"

"No, as in a big truck."

She laughed. "I see that bang on your head did nothing to improve your disposition."

"Well, quite frankly, I'd like to get out of 'dis' position, if you don't mind."

"I'm not stopping you." She kept her voice low.

Oh, but you are, dear heart. You are. He could feel her gentle breath upon his face, she sat so close to him. He couldn't seem to turn from the merriment reflected in her green eyes. And besides all that, she was now leaning on his shirt-sleeve. He tugged his arm free. "There, now I can move."

"I'm sorry. I didn't realize I was on your arm."

"No harm done." *None at all, if you don't count causing me to think of things I shouldn't be thinking of. Things like how to kiss you right now.* Moving cautiously, he managed to sit up without too much pain.

"Is anything hurt?"

"Just my ego." He had begun to remember what happened. "I've never had an accident out here before."

"It wasn't your fault, you know."

Could he hear concern in her voice? He expected her to reiterate exactly how dangerous this trip was and to chastise him, but she refrained. "I should have kept a closer watch on things."

"Everything worked out okay—as long as you're not hurt."

Could this be the same woman he'd been traveling with for the past eight days? The same woman who turned everything into an argument spurred on by fear? He shook his head, then instantly regretted the movement. "I'll be sore for a few days, but I'm fine. Tell me what happened."

"You don't remember being in the flood?"

"No, I'm Moses, remember? Noah was in the flood." He tried not to smile at the shock that registered on her face, but her expression was so lovely he couldn't resist.

She sighed like a longsuffering saint. "I see."

"Said the blind man as he picked up his hammer and saw."

Stephanie giggled, a musical sound to his ears. "Yes, you are in top form today," she said. "Anyway, you were rescuing Paula when you were knocked out. Ian had to jump in to save you."

"I don't remember any of that."

"Of course not, you were unconscious."

"Guess that ancient Chinese proverb isn't true for me."

"Which one is that?"

"Throw a lucky man in the river, and he will come up with a fish in his mouth. I don't see any fish, so—"

"Where do you get all these silly lines?"

"I'm beginning to think I have too much time on my hands," he confessed to her with a grin. Time he'd suddenly like to spend with her. He loved this softer side. Could it be she had finally decided to let go of her worries and hurts and give them to God?

"You've only just figured that out? I've known it all along."

"Guess I need a good woman to help me occupy my time." He winked at her. *Take it slow*, he said to himself. *Wait for God's leading.*

"I think any woman could help you occupy your free time."

"Does that mean you're applying for the job?" Okay, so he wasn't listening to his own logic. His heart had decided to take over.

"Job? Is it that much work to help you fill your time?"

"I'm sure a ten-day trek to the desert and then coming home to tend to our dozen or so children will keep you pretty busy." *Slow down!*

"What's the pay?"

"All the love and kisses you could ever want." He ran his fingers through her hair. *Lord, am I in over my head? If so, you'll have to rescue me. I'm caught up in feelings of love for this woman.*

She smiled and placed her hand over his. "While it's an opportunity I can't afford to pass up since I'd be the richest woman alive, I do think we need to have a date first."

"We've already had one date. We'll have a long engagement." Steph giggled.

"You seem more alive today than I've ever seen you."

"A few minutes ago, as I was looking around, I felt like Dorothy in the *Wizard of Oz*. All my life, everything has been in black and white. Then this morning, it appears as though my whole world has shifted to Technicolor. It's the most beautiful thing."

"Well, I can assure you, Dorothy, you're not in Kansas anymore."

"Really? So are you the Tin Man who doesn't have a heart, the Scarecrow who doesn't have a brain, or the Cowardly Lion?"

"I'm the Wizard, and I'm going to take you home." He winced as he shifted. "Close your eyes, tap your heels three times, and say 'There's no place like home.' " When Stephanie did as he said, he leaned forward, despite the pain, and tenderly kissed her on the mouth.

When he stopped kissing her, she opened her eyes. "I've never felt so at home as I do with you right now."

"Then it worked," he said, cupping her chin in his hand.

"Hey, Uncle Nate is awake!" Keith shouted and jumped out of his sleeping bag.

Within minutes, everyone crowded close, asking questions all at once. Nate could feel his head spinning from the excitement. How he longed for a few more minutes alone with Stephanie.

After breakfast and the best-tasting coffee he had had so far, they sat and discussed what to do. Eventually, they reached a difficult decision. Due to the flood and their injuries, they would not continue. Nathan was certain he saw tears in Steph's eyes when the final vote was cast.

Once they gathered up everything and lowered themselves from the ledge, they disbanded to clean up. Nathan spoke quietly with Stephanie for a few moments.

"They did a great job, didn't they?"

"I'm very proud of them." She gazed fondly at the group.

"I feel the same. Of them and you. Will they visit us after we're married?"

"Married? Who said anything about marriage? That must have been some knock on the head."

He swallowed hard. *Had it all been a dream?* "What? What do you mean?"

"I can't even stand the desert. Why would I marry someone who lives in it 90 percent of his life?"

"But you said—"

"You were rather delirious last night, Nathan. I'm afraid you're mistaken."

He could feel a crushing tightness in his chest—the very heart that overflowed with love for her. He didn't know how he'd fallen so hard, but that didn't matter. "I—I see," he stammered, desperately trying to remember if their conversation had been a dream or not.

"Said the blind man as he saw his hammer."

Nathan burst out laughing. "No, no. Picked up his hammer and saw. Get it? Why, you little munchkin! I wasn't dreaming."

"You may not be, but I feel like I am."

She stepped forward and brushed his cheek with her lips.

Lord, if this is what heaven is like here on earth, I may never want to leave!

ten

Stephanie could tell it pained Nathan deeply to have to end the camp. She admired him for the way he handled the disappointment, and she wished she could do something to ease the ache he must be feeling. A large lump had formed on the side of his head, and welts and bruises covered his arms and shoulders, yet he never complained.

Paula kept up a brave front as well, despite her injuries. Aside from the almost embarrassing display of thanks she gave Nathan for saving her life, she seemed fine.

As Stephanie watched the group, everyone appeared to be moving slower. Were they all as disappointed as Nathan, or were they just weary from the previous day's events? Talking had been reduced to a minimum, and now it was Paula's pack hanging from the staff. Nathan still managed to carry his.

He had spare batteries in his pack and tried to make radio contact after the vote, but to no avail. Since they were in no condition to climb, they trudged back to the last oasis. Once there, they could get fresh water, and Nathan would try to radio for help again. At least it would be easier for Jim to spot them.

Damian walked by himself, scowling. He hadn't said much this morning but had appeared delighted to learn of their retreat from the desert. The more Steph got to know about the man, the more she disliked him.

The opposite was true of Nathan. This morning he had handed her some slices of dried apple, and she blushed as she remembered the verse from the night before: *"Refresh me with apples, for I am faint with love."*

Now the lighthearted moments from the morning had faded and everyone marched silently. Nathan showed up at Stephanie's side, matching her dampened pace. Eventually, he broke the silence.

"I think yesterday was a turning point for these kids."

"How so?"

"Now you, being a professional and all, might disagree with me here, but in this country we have no ritual that marks when a boy becomes a man. Well, except for the Bar Mitzvah for Jewish boys. For the rest of us, there is no 'coming of age point,' if you will, to signify that we're no longer children and now have a responsibility to ourselves and our community to become productive citizens.

"But yesterday these kids had a major test to pass. They had to survive, as well as help others to survive."

Steph smiled. "They never once questioned that, either. When Heather panicked, they all pitched in to help her."

"So I heard. What they learned will stay with them a long time. And, hopefully, when it seems that the waters are about to overflow again, they'll know they can handle anything."

She nodded in agreement. "I am reminded of that verse of Scripture you used when we first met. The one about training a child."

"Exactly."

"I want to thank you for yesterday."

"Thank me for nearly drowning?"

"No, for talking to me about God. You helped to remove a brick from that wall I had put up between Him and myself. Then when the flood hit, the wall came tumbling down, and I began to pray."

"I'm glad to hear that. But somehow I knew it. I vaguely recall someone sitting with me all night quoting Scripture. I thought I had dreamed it." He smiled and took her hand as they continued to walk.

"You've helped all of us on this trip," Steph said.

"And what about your decision?"

"Despite how poorly things ended up for us here, I think it's a great idea. I'm wondering if ten days is a little too long. Would you consider a compromise?"

Nathan squeezed her hand gently. "You're wonderful, do you know that?"

"They don't think I'm very wonderful now, suggesting we turn back like this." She nodded toward the rest of the group.

"Don't be so hard on yourself. We voted."

"It's kind of sad, really."

"That we didn't get to the end?"

"I've finally started to see the beauty you claim is here. We were becoming a family in a way. A family I don't have."

"It feels good to connect with others. You've been withdrawn too long, Steph. It's great to have you back."

"I don't mind telling you it's nice to be back." She bit her lip. She still needed to tell Nathan the rest of her story, but everything between them was so wonderful right now she didn't want to spoil it. She hoped when she did tell him, he would still feel the same about her. "I'll never stop thanking God for this trip."

Nathan slapped his hand on his thigh and laughed. "And I bet you thought you'd never say that."

"Oh, ye of little faith."

"Now, see, that's where you're wrong. I had faith you'd come around."

"Thank you," she whispered, wishing she could express her feelings better.

The beleaguered group traveled on. When they stopped for their afternoon break, Stephanie asked Nathan to say something to boost morale.

"Now I know it's been disappointing to have to turn back, but your guide is pretty beaten up."

"You don't look so bad, Uncle Nate," Keith called out.

"Glad to hear it. I've got some things I'd like to say about yesterday, and then we won't bring up the subject again—unless you want to. Is that okay?"

"Shoot," said Tom.

"First off, kudos to you, Ian, for deciding on climbing the mesa. If we'd taken our usual route, we all might have been seriously injured in the flood. So a round of applause for our leader Ian."

Everyone cheered and patted him on the back.

"Second. Paula, you were incredibly brave and strong out there. I don't know how you held on to that rock, but I'm so glad you did."

I know how, thought Stephanie.

Paula blushed. "How could all of that happen so fast?"

"It's not uncommon. When the rain pours down it doesn't seep into the ground like normal soil. It's pretty amazing—not to mention scary—to see."

"Even scarier to be involved in," Keith said.

"All I heard was like this animal roar and then *bam!*" Paula clapped her palms together.

"I've seen worse flash floods than that. In less than a minute, I've seen a dry bed fill to over eight feet high."

"If we didn't have injured parties in our group," Liz ventured cautiously, "would we still have had to turn back? I mean, would there have been more flash floods, do you think?"

"We probably would have kept going. We were heading for higher ground, and the water had receded by then." He looked around at the fallen faces. "But that doesn't mean we may not have had to turn back a little farther," he added quickly. "Now I haven't talked this over with Miss H., but maybe we could do this again."

"The whole thing?" asked Heather, who seemed almost disappointed.

"Sure."

It appeared to Stephanie that everyone but Heather cheered. Perhaps yesterday had been more traumatic for her than Steph realized.

"So that means you'll be doing this camp on a regular basis for those of us who need to be straightened out?" Heather said.

"I wouldn't put it that way. The purpose of this trip is to help you learn about teamwork and self-assurance. In this day and age, everyone seems to be out for himself. I wanted to show you how capable you are and what could be achieved by working together." Nathan offered the girl a smile. "I don't think any one of you needed straightening out, as you put it. I'm thoroughly impressed with each of you."

Stephanie stepped forward. "Nathan's right, Heather. You did a great job out there working together, and you saw how essential your effort was."

"I was afraid."

"We all were," Stephanie replied. "The important thing is you didn't panic, and you got the job done."

As the conversation moved on to other things, Stephanie had an uneasy feeling in the pit of her stomach. Something wasn't right with Heather, but she couldn't pinpoint the problem.

"What would have happened if you had stayed unconscious?" Ian asked.

Nathan smiled. "Me? Out for the count? Not on your life. But when we didn't show up at the pick-up point in two days, they would have come looking for us. Plus my buddy Jim checks on us often. When I'm on a long trip, it's difficult to carry all the food, so he even drops supplies at certain times and check points for me—kind of like manna from heaven."

Stephanie laughed. This was becoming more like a biblical story than she had envisioned.

"Huh? What's manna from heaven?" Liz wanted to know.

"Let's take a break," Nathan said, removing his pack carefully. He gave a brief reply to Liz's question, but most of them had never heard of the story, so he sat down at their urging and told them about Moses, the plagues, the Ten Commandments, and the forty years in the desert. He had their rapt attention.

"Okay, if you're this Moses fellow, I wanna know why you didn't just part the waters for you and Paula?" Keith asked.

Nathan and Stephanie exchanged glances.

"I didn't say I *was* Moses," he explained.

"Well, if you were, I'd rewrite those commandments you were telling me about. And the first one would be 'Thou shalt not wade in a dry ditch during a rainstorm in the desert.'"

"Hey!" Paula said with a pout.

"No, the first one would be 'Thou shalt not carry a radio

and not tell anyone else!'" Ian said.

"Enough. This is getting out of hand," Nathan interjected.

"We've got plenty more, Uncle Nate," Liz offered.

Stephanie viewed the whole scene with delight as Nathan blushed from their playful taunts. When he finally got them to stop teasing, she felt like she'd watched a ringmaster working the crowd. There were certainly many sides to be discovered about this man she had fallen for in a big way.

Then a thought struck her. *What if this isn't Your will, Lord?*

20

The hike back to the last oasis stretched on and on, but Stephanie appreciated the time she had with Nathan. They talked about so many things, and a bond of trust seemed to be forming. At least it felt that way.

She had never allowed herself to become close to anyone. Not by conscious choice—it just sort of happened that way. In school, getting her psychology degree, they all had to take therapy, and for some reason her problem with intimacy never came up.

"You're awfully quiet," Nathan said, breaking their long silence.

"Hmm."

"Something or someone?"

She rolled her eyes. "Someone."

"Good," he whispered in her ear.

His breath tickled. "What makes you think it's you I'm thinking about?"

"No one else could put such satisfaction on your face." He slipped his fingers through hers.

"My, we really do have a high opinion of ourself. Guess my original diagnosis stands."

"And what diagnosis would that be?"

"Egomaniac."

"Then you'll have your work cut out for you for the next forty or fifty years."

"You think there's hope for you?" she said, enjoying their banter.

"Only with you by my side."

"I can see an improvement already!" She squeezed his fingers gently.

"B–b–baby, you ain't seen nothin' yet," he tried to sing to her.

She laughed and walked closer to him.

As they neared the oasis, she couldn't help but remember the spot where he had washed her hair. She could feel her pulse quicken. The event, though innocent enough, had taken on a whole new meaning for her now.

Thinking back to the New Testament when Jesus washed the disciples' feet, she visualized Nathan's washing of her hair as his way of showing he was a servant. He willingly served God with his business. The act also showed that he was willing to attend to her—despite all her resistance and anger toward him. Despite her fears that once he knew the whole truth, his feelings for her would change—dramatically.

On some other level, though, she felt it showed his compassion and concern for her. Maybe he didn't understand what a woman went through without benefit of a shower and hairdryer, but he took the time to help make it better for her anyway. As she remembered other events of the trip, she saw his empathy displayed in so many forms with each of them.

Late in the day they settled about two hundred yards from the oasis. Stephanie was never so relieved to put down her pack. Without the weight, her shoulders felt as if they were floating upward.

Sighs of repose from the weary travelers replaced the usual chatter. At least they would get one more night together.

Surely she could find a way to brighten the mood. Glancing around, she spotted where they had made a water still and then carefully filled in the hole. Nathan never liked to disturb the natural habitat of the desert. He did so only when necessary and to help them learn.

Thus, they carried their own wood for the nights they had a campfire. They kept all their garbage with them and trod carefully.

As she smiled at the memories being played like a video in her mind, she wondered where Nathan had gotten the cactus for the water still. And, more important, where he had put it when they were finished.

Hmmm, I have an idea. Perhaps a little fun with Nathan would cheer up this sad group.

"Did you hear me?" Nathan asked as he stood over her.

"I'm sorry. I must have been lost in thought." She could feel herself blush.

"I'm going to take a little walk." He knelt close to her and whispered, "The plane will be by soon, and I want to try the radio. Hopefully, it will work, and I can tell Jim what's happened so he can send someone for us. I don't want the group to hear. Keep them with you, if you can."

Oh, Nathan, you are so thoughtful I could kiss you. "Okay," she replied with a smile she hoped spoke of her new feelings of love for him.

As soon as he was out of earshot, she gathered everyone around her. "Who wants to have fun with Nathan?"

All the kids nodded eagerly.

"Anyone know what he did with that cactus from the still?"

"I think it's in his pack," replied Liz.

"Good. Is there a lot of it?"

"No, only a little," answered Paula. "But he found a damaged cactus yesterday and picked it up, too."

"We could cut some more," Heather offered.

"No. Nathan said the cactus is protected, and we can't damage it," Tom explained.

"How much does he have?" Stephanie asked.

"A full bag, I think," Paula said, looking puzzled.

"Oh, this is great! Someone needs to find the cactus in his pack. Then, when he's pulled out his sleeping bag for bed, we need to fill it with the cactus."

"That won't work," Ian said. "He always checks his bag before getting in, remember? Like we all should be doing."

"You're right. Okay, so we let him check his bag, then we

distract him. How do we do that?" A little bit of excitement rose in Stephanie's stomach.

"Someone could ask him to come look at something."

"Good idea, Heather." It pleased Stephanie to see the girl getting involved. "Would you like to try and divert him?"

Heather nodded shyly.

The prank was small and silly, but dreaming it up seemed to bring back a few smiles. Now all they had to do was wait until Nathan finished his radio call, then readied for bed.

The air of defeat had turned to one of anticipation.

❧

"No, nothing major, Jim. I think I reinjured my rotator cuff. Over."

The radio crackled. "We'll be out first thing in the morning to get all of you. Over."

"Right. Over and out."

As Nathan clicked off the radio, the plane rose higher into the sky and soon vanished from view. He hated to do this. Even Jim had been surprised. But it had to be done, since neither he nor Paula were in any shape to carry their load.

Sitting down on a rock formation, he pondered the day's events. *Lord, my heart is heavy when I should be rejoicing. Every time I think of Stephanie, it is such a rush for me. Thank You for bringing her into my life.* Nathan released a heavy sigh. *I'm feeling weighted down, Lord. And something tells me this mood is more than sadness over having to return. Please guide me so that I can keep everyone safe.*

He rubbed his throbbing shoulder then tried to improve his range of motion by rotating it slowly.

Feeling heavy-hearted, Nathan trudged back to the group. He noticed a lot of whispering and snickering going on when he arrived but pretended not to. No doubt Keith was up to something.

When he looked over at Stephanie, he saw a small grin play across her face. *Stephanie*, he thought, *what have you got planned? It's a good thing I love you, Lady.*

Stephanie spotted Nathan first. "Shush, he's coming."

Everyone scattered and quickly pretended to be doing something. Stephanie noticed their actions were more pronounced, their laughter forced. Actors they weren't.

When Nathan headed in her direction, she could hardly keep from smiling. *Yeah, criticize the others, but you're not any better at it!*

"Everything go all right?" she asked, trying to sound casual.

"Yep," Nathan replied, looking around.

"So what's next?"

"They'll be here in the morning to take us back."

Steph placed her hands over his. "It's okay. They understand." She studied the look in his eyes for a moment and then glanced away, wishing she could comfort him somehow.

"Perhaps we should all try to hit the hay early tonight. Maybe a good night's sleep will help," Nathan said.

"Good idea. Okay, I'm going to the oasis. Don't send the troops out to find me," she teased, remembering what happened when she left the group without telling anyone.

"Let me know if that little shrew made it home, will ya?" Keith hollered. "I searched for him on the way back but couldn't find him."

"I'll do my best."

"Want some company?" Nathan asked as she turned to leave.

"Do I have a choice?"

"Oh, the pain." He covered his heart with his hands.

"If you put it that way, I suppose I'll let you join me."

"Are you going for a walk, or were you going to try and sneak a bath?"

"Mostly for a walk." How could she tell him she wanted to be alone to think about him and remember their first visit to the oasis?

"Tell me about your family," Nathan asked while they walked away from the others.

"Haven't I told you everything?"

"Some. But not nearly enough."

"Did I tell you I had two sisters?" Her voice cracked.

He took her hand in his. "Were they older?"

"Gloria was, and so beautiful she could have been a model. But she wanted to be a lawyer. I think she would have been good at it, too. I lost every fight we had."

"I find that hard to believe. Have I won any we've had?"

"Very funny."

"I thought so."

"Joy, the youngest, was such a sweet kid. Barely in her teens, but the boys all loved her. She had a killer sense of humor. Sometimes Keith reminds me of her."

"It's still hard for you, isn't it?"

"Is it easy for you?"

"Easier," he said sadly. "I don't remember my family."

"I'm being selfish. I'm sorry."

They reached the oasis and sat down. Moonlight glistened on the water, and the sounds of wildlife rustled in the cottonwood trees.

"Don't be. I think it's good to talk about them. It keeps your memories alive."

"I can still see Joy running home from grade school all excited. She burst into the house and said, 'Fannie, Fannie, Luke gave me his gum.' I didn't understand her excitement at first until she explained he'd passed it to her when they kissed."

Nathan laughed heartily.

"Joy lived life to the fullest." She stopped. Nathan was still laughing. "What? It wasn't that funny."

"Oh, yes, it was. *Fannie.*"

Her face turned hot with embarrassment. She hadn't even realized what she'd said. "If you tell anyone my nickname, I'll have you committed."

"Whatever you say, Fannie," he said as he nuzzled her neck.

"Stop that!"

"Okay," he obliged, pulling away from her.

"I meant stop calling me Fannie."

"I will erase it from my memory bank if you kiss me."

"A single kiss?"

"Hmm, maybe two." He tapped his finger on his chin, as if contemplating whether that would be enough to silence him.

"Only two kisses?"

"How about an even four?"

"Do I have your word? I mean, it's not like I can get the negatives from you or anything. In fact, what's to stop you from blackmailing me all my life?"

"Nothing." He grinned in mock wickedness.

"Where's a time travel machine when you need one?" She jumped up and started to walk. "Ah, I think we should be getting back."

Nathan quickly followed. "But we didn't finish negotiating."

"I've decided it doesn't matter if everyone knows my nickname." *Perhaps some reverse psychology might help.*

"Should I call your bluff?"

"Don't you have some sort of parable to draw from in this instance?"

"Actually, I'm kinda at a loss for words," he admitted.

"My, my. Won't everyone be surprised to hear that?"

"Your terms?"

"I say nothing about your current speechless situation nor explain to everyone what you were mumbling in your sleep last night. In return, you tell no one about my nickname."

"You drive a hard bargain. Do I at least find out what I said while delirious?"

"That's not on the table at this point." It felt good to have the upper hand.

"Now what's to stop you from blackmailing me all my life?"

"Good question."

"That's not an answer, you know."

"We're almost back at the camp. Do we have a deal?" She stopped walking.

"Do we shake on it?"

"Are we back to answering questions with questions?"

"What do you think?"

"I think you'd better seal the deal now." She pointed to the seven pairs of eyes watching them.

"Deal," he whispered. "We'll settle up later."

She couldn't wait.

❧

Steph's thoughts remained on Nathan when he came over to say good night.

"I guess I shouldn't have kept you so long at the oasis. You hardly slept at all last night, watching over me. Aren't you tired?"

"Actually, I'm doing okay. Every time I've felt too tired to go on, I've prayed."

"Isn't God good? I'm so thankful He brought you into my life." He raised her hands and kissed them.

"And I'm thankful for you. More than you'll ever know." She fought back tears of joy and silently prayed he would still feel the same once the whole truth came out.

"Now, Lady, time for some sleep. I must say you look lovely even with that raccoon-like appearance." He pointed to her eyes.

"I won't argue with you this time," she said in surrender.

"What? That shrew really did steal your tongue. I've never known you not to argue with me."

"Nothing lasts forever."

"But our love will. Good night." He finally released her hands then held her sleeping bag open for her to crawl into.

When he walked away, Stephanie quickly opened her eyes. She had nearly fallen asleep in the second or two they were shut. *Guess I am tired. But I need to stay awake and see what happens.*

She waited long, breathless minutes before Nathan finally pulled out his sleeping bag, shook it out, and laid it on the ground. As he started to climb in, Heather came running back from the direction of the oasis.

"Nathan, come quick!" she shouted.

He jumped up and ran to her. "What's the problem?"

"Back at the oasis, there's an injured animal. You've got to help him."

Heather's acting impressed Steph. In fact, she wondered if perhaps the girl spoke the truth.

"I don't know if I can—"

Heather reached out and grabbed Nathan by the arm. "You've got to come."

As the two of them rushed toward the oasis, Liz and Keith quickly placed all the cactus pieces in Nathan's sleeping bag.

"Look, there's a lump!" Liz cried.

"So I'll move it. Don't panic," Keith responded.

Stephanie fought the slumber she yearned for, trying to stay awake for Nathan's return. But it was hard. Too hard, and sleep finally won.

Sobbing woke Stephanie abruptly. She sat up and gazed about with bleary eyes. Heather! She unzipped her sleeping bag and raced to the girl's side.

"What's the matter?" She could see a tear in the shoulder of Heather's cotton shirt, and several buttons were missing. Had there really been an animal? Had it been so frightened it tore the teen's shirt trying to get away?

Heather only wailed louder in response to Stephanie's question. By now the others were awake and standing nearby.

"Where's Nathan?" Stephanie asked, looking around for him.

Still no reply, only sobs.

"Was there really an animal?"

Heather shook her head.

"Tell me, Heather. I can't help you if I don't know what has happened." Stephanie cradled the upset girl in her arms.

"He, Nathan, he—made a pass at me," Heather managed to choke out.

"What?" Stephanie felt a shock reverberate through her whole body.

"Nathan. He tried to kiss me. When I slapped him, he tore my clothes."

Stephanie opened her mouth, but no words came out.

"Are you sure?" Liz asked.

Paula folded her arms. "I can't believe that."

"Damian, will you go find Nathan, please?" Stephanie asked.

"I don't think we want him back at the camp after this," Damian said.

"Do it," Stephanie ordered while still embracing Heather.

"You don't have to shout," he mumbled as a parting comment.

"Okay, can I have some privacy, gang? I'd like to talk with Heather. Alone."

The youths disbanded, leaving Stephanie and Heather to talk. She pulled the girl over to sit on her sleeping bag.

"Tell me exactly what happened."

"Nathan followed me to the oasis, and when I got there I pretended I couldn't find the wounded animal. When he looked around he said, 'There was nothing here, was there? You wanted to be alone with me.' I tried to tell him no, but he grabbed me and tried to kiss me. I fought him off, and when I got free he tore my clothing."

Stephanie didn't know what to do. She knew in her heart Nathan would never do such a thing. And then the thought hit her as the old doubts and fears assailed her. *Is this a sign, Lord? I asked You to show me if I was doing the right thing.*

Pulling a tissue from her pack, Steph dabbed at Heather's tears. "It's okay. Everything will be all right. Let's get you changed."

Time dragged while Stephanie tried to calm Heather. Eventually the girl drifted off to sleep, exhausted. Through it all, Steph's concentration was divided. She wondered where Damian and Nathan were. She desperately needed to hear Nathan's side of the story.

"Liz, will you keep an eye on Heather for me?" she asked as she left to go in search of the two missing men.

eleven

Stephanie had only taken a few steps away from the camp when she met up with Nathan and Damian. Neither of them spoke for a moment.

"What happened?" she asked through tight lips, her hands on her hips.

"According to Damian, Heather gave you all the details." Nathan spoke calmly.

"I want to hear your side of the story, Nathan."

"I trust Heather to give you the truth."

"Heather is distraught and can hardly speak. Can't you tell me what went on here?"

"Heather will tell you when she's able." He walked past her without further comment.

Stephanie felt her knees weaken. Heather had already told her side of the story. Surely he must know what she had said. *I don't know what to do.* She turned around to follow him. "Is that all you're going to say?" Her voice quivered with emotion.

Nathan only nodded.

"Under the circumstances, Miss Harris, I think it's good we are being picked up in the morning, wouldn't you say?" Damian's words belied the seriousness of the situation. He actually sounded pleased. Surely this would wound Nathan. Would he speak up now?

Silence.

"You've nothing else to say, Nathan?" Stephanie looked pleadingly at him, but he turned away. What could she do? "I'll expect you and Damian to stay on the far side of the camp. Under no circumstances do either of you approach any females."

"That goes without saying, Miss Harris. But I resent being included in this." Damian folded his arms and appeared ready to throw a temper tantrum.

"It's only a precaution for your own safety, Damian," Nathan said in a tone barely audible. By the moonlight, Stephanie could see that his face had paled, almost ghost-like, devoid of life. Exactly like how she felt inside.

"Good night," she said and walked back to her sleeping bag, her foot hurting with every step. Lying in the dark with her back to the group, she listened to the evening sounds of the desert. She fought the heaviness in her heart and the weight of her tired eyelids. Yet sleep evaded her. She tossed and turned and worried about Nathan and Heather.

Her prayers seemed to evaporate from her lips, and she doubted if God could even hear them. Heaven seemed too far away. When she opened her eyes and looked at the tall saguaro cactus nearby, she felt a deep loss. In the light of the moon, the saguaro seemed to be stretching its limbs heavenward. She remembered a sermon about surrendering to God by raising your arms in such a way.

She strained to remember more verses of Scripture, but tonight nothing would come to mind. She felt crushed beneath the weight of the events and begged God to help her understand what had taken place.

"Miss H., you still awake?" Keith whispered as he approached and squatted beside her.

"Yes."

"I took the cactus out of Nathan's bed."

"Thanks."

"You know, Nathan would never do what Heather said he did. I just know it. What did he say when you asked him?"

She pushed herself up and rested on her elbow. "I can't discuss that right now."

"Know what I think? I think he wants her to take responsibility for the things she said."

Steph remained silent.

"That's what this camp is about, isn't it? Being accountable for our own actions. Whether they are good or bad."

"Yes, Keith, you're right."

"So now what do we do?"

"We go home in the morning."

He shifted his weight as he crouched. "And what will happen to Nathan?"

"I'm not sure."

"Should we tell Heather we don't believe her? We know Uncle Nate? He would never do this."

Steph felt herself choke for a moment as despair tore at her heart. "I think it would be wise not to discuss the matter. You may be called upon to make a statement. I don't want to influence you or anyone else in any way. If any of the others start to talk about it, please advise them to stop."

"Good idea, Miss H. Thanks."

"And, Keith, please say a prayer for both of them tonight." *Where did that come from?* How could she ask someone to pray when she couldn't?

"You got it," he said, pointing two thumbs up. "Night, Miss H. Stop worrying and get some sleep."

"Thanks. I'll try." But Stephanie knew sleep would elude her like the happiness she had so desperately sought since the loss of her family.

Finally, when she thought the long, lonely nights were over, it looked as if they were only going to get worse. Better if she had never met Nathan Moses. Things had been fine until the day she laid eyes on him.

How can you say that? a small voice asked her. *Only moments ago you were praising God for bringing him into your life. Now you're cursing the day you met him.*

"Arrggghh," she growled as she rolled over the other way. If only she had something to hit.

⁓

Nathan's head pounded. The pain had dimmed to a dull ache before the incident with Heather. But when she clobbered him with her fist and he fell, the throbbing had started again full force.

He knew he had handled things badly. Seeing Damian approach as he came to could only mean things were worse than he initially thought.

Damian yelled at him, asking if he'd lost his mind, babbling on about Heather being upset and sobbing. What else could he have expected her to say? His rejection had caused her pain and embarrassment. He tried to explain everything to Heather, but she had refused to listen.

Now, as he lay awake, watching the clear sky and twinkling stars, he wished he knew what to do to make this situation better for everyone.

He had not wanted to contradict whatever Heather said to hide her embarrassment, but after Damian's outburst, he realized she'd accused him of something much worse than rejection.

Seeing the agony on Stephanie's face this evening was the worst thing he'd ever had to endure. He yearned to tell her everything, but he had to give Heather a chance first. Wasn't that what this excursion was all about?

Glancing at his watch, Nathan realized that in a few hours he'd be leaving the desert—probably for the last time. The only life he'd ever really known had come to a close. Even if the girl did tell the truth, he'd never get the state contract now.

The life he'd hoped to share with Steph had also slipped from his grasp. This thought cut the deepest and tore at his insides worse than the raging waters in the flood. For like Moses, Nathan would never reach the land flowing with milk and honey. The little piece of heaven here on earth that he'd already tasted would never be his.

A solitary teardrop slipped slowly down his cheek. He swiped at it with the back of his hand. *Where do I go from here, Lord? I'll trust You have something better. But could anything be better than Stephanie?* The beauty of the desert paled compared to her.

Would he trade the desert, the night sky, and everything else he'd ever known for her? In a second. Like he'd said before, what good is it all if you don't have anyone to share it with?

He took in a deep breath then exhaled. All that he had worked so hard to gain had been lost in a split second.

Everything. Including Stephanie. What would tomorrow bring? Where would he go? Only God knew.

⁂

Stephanie awoke with a start, the back of her head wet with sweat. Her breathing felt erratic as she focused on her room. She stared at her alarm clock. Nearly three in the morning.

It had been four days since her return from the desert, and every night had been the same. She was awake more than asleep. If this continued, she'd have to see a doctor.

Each time she closed her eyes, Steph could see Nathan's face. His eyes were filled with despair, and the images tormented her. Guilt stabbed her heart as she recounted the events over and over.

How could she have had him arrested and charged? She believed in his innocence, but she had a duty. She could not take child protection concerns lightly and still keep her job.

When she squeezed her eyes shut again, she began to cry. Tiny sobs escaped. She tried to think of other things, but always she came back to Nathan. Buried in pain and turmoil, hurting for Nathan as well as herself, she wondered, *How can I go back to my old life after all this?*

⁂

"What are you doing here?" Phil said as he entered her office. "You look terrible. You're supposed to be home."

Stephanie could hardly answer. "I need to be doing something."

"Did something else happen out there besides the incident with Heather?"

She shook her head but then started to cry. Wasn't she all cried out yet?

"This is no place for you. I'm taking you home."

Steph couldn't reply. She merely nodded, picked up her purse, and followed Phil out of her office. Though he spoke to her secretary, she didn't really hear anything he said.

"I'll get someone to follow me to your place tonight, and I'll drop off your car. You won't be needing it since I'm ordering you straight to bed when you get home."

"Okay," she whispered.

"When you're feeling better, we can talk about things. For now, take a few days to rest. Unless there's something I should know right now?"

Steph merely shook her head.

"Of course, if you want to say you told me so, now would be a good time. I feel awful."

She knew Phil was trying to make her feel better, but nothing he could say would help. The more solicitous he became, the more disheartened she grew.

After driving her home, he walked her to her apartment and unlocked the door. As he handed back her key, he placed one hand under her chin and lifted it so her eyes met his. "Steph, I've never seen you like this. Do you need a doctor?"

"Give me a few days. I—I'll be fine," she choked out.

"Something is terribly wrong. I can see it in your eyes. Can't you tell me what it is?"

Her bottom lip quivered. "Later."

"I'll call you tomorrow."

"Thanks," she replied shakily.

"Anytime." He backed away, waving to her.

She closed the door. Never had the gaping hole in her heart seemed so big. Phil reminded her of the father she had lost. If her father had been here, she could have gone to him and told him what happened. Not having him available seemed only to magnify the ache.

And now, with Nathan, it felt like losing her family all over again.

❧

For two days, Stephanie didn't leave her apartment or make contact with anyone. Phil, Rachel, and Damian all called, but she did not phone them back.

How she wished Nathan would call, but she knew he wouldn't. He had barely spoken to her the next day. He didn't even look at her when she left him at the police station. For all she knew, he was still incarcerated.

Everyone probably knew Heather's story wasn't true, but she couldn't do anything about it. Nathan had refused to contradict Heather, and without two sides to a story, that left only one version for Stephanie to act upon.

Sitting up in her bed, hugging her knees, Steph prayed God would work a miracle. When she finished, she padded to the bathroom to take a shower.

While the hot water pulsated on her back, she thought about Nathan and wondered how his injured shoulder was faring.

As she stepped out of the shower, she heard the phone ringing but let the answering machine get it. She wrapped a towel around herself and listened to the tape.

"Hi, Steph, it's me. It's Friday night. Where are we going? Give me a call at work. I'll pick you up, if you want. Let me know, okay?"

Steph stood staring at the phone for several minutes. She and Rachel had gone out every Friday night for as long as she could remember. They'd always agreed no man would ever come between them, yet Stephanie wanted to be with Nathan. Since that wasn't possible, she didn't want to be with anyone. How could she explain that to Rachel without hurting her feelings?

Steph turned on her computer and sent an e-mail message telling Rachel she wasn't able to go out. It wasn't really a lie. After all, she still wasn't sleeping much.

The morning dragged on, and she grew restless. She tried reading a magazine but tossed it aside. She visited Nathan's website several times, typing out long messages and then clicking delete instead of send.

Her appetite had all but left her. For lunch she ate some stale popcorn while watching a movie on TV. She drifted off to sleep before the show ended. It was a welcome rest, but it didn't last.

In the early evening, she got dressed and walked over to the corner store. The clerk nodded his head when she entered.

"Have you got something for insomnia?" she asked.

"Over there on the back wall," he replied, pointing her in the right direction.

"Miss Harris, how nice to see you."

Stephanie froze. Damian. *Why the big smile?* she wondered. "What are you doing here?"

"Believe it or not, I thought I'd pick up two cups of coffee before I came to see you. What can I get you?"

She shook her head. "See me? Why?"

He leaned against a magazine rack. "Have you spoken with Nathan?"

"No." She could feel her pulse quicken.

"He has agreed to sell me his company. He's leaving town."

"He can't do that. Doesn't he know the consequences of failing to appear?" Stephanie cringed at the thought.

Damian shrugged.

"Why did he sell the business?"

"I made him an offer he couldn't refuse."

Not Nathan. He wouldn't sell out for money. His company meant too much to him. A throbbing pulse hammered at her temples. Something wasn't right. "How long have you two been partners?"

Damian laughed. "We never were quite partners. I had offered, but he hadn't accepted. Now I've bought him outright. It's best this way. And I'm not interested in a state contract if that's what's worrying you."

"Have you any idea how much work he put into that business or how important it was to him?" Stephanie glanced around at the few people in the store. She had raised her voice a little louder than she intended and didn't care for the unwanted attention.

"It can't be that important if he sold it to me."

"Does he know you lied to me?" She folded her arms.

"Of course not. And I didn't lie."

"Just not the whole truth, is that what you're saying? I don't believe I've ever met a more selfish person than you."

"Now hold on there. I helped Nathan out."

"And how did you help him? Did you pay Heather for her little charade, too?"

Damian looked surprised by her comments. "Maybe I didn't care for the man or his stupid survival camp, but I'd never stoop that low. I'm a businessman, and this was strictly business."

"Was it business to kick him when he was down? Couldn't you at least have stood by him through this?" She knew her anger should be directed at herself as well.

"I don't see you sticking by him."

Damian's words cut deep. How could she stand by someone who probably hated her? She saw the look in Nathan's eyes when he was arrested. She knew he'd never forgive her. "No, I don't suppose you do."

"Look, I meant no harm to Nathan," Damian said in a softer tone. "You've got to believe me. He's actually an okay guy. He's strong. He'll find something else he loves. His kind always do. Life always seems to work out for them."

She glared at him. "You think being orphaned at a young age and then running away from a group home at twelve are breaks in life?"

"Of course not. But some old geezer gave him a great life and money, too."

"Mr. Moses wasn't rich. Nathan had to work hard to build his business. It wasn't handed to him, unlike someone else I know. Oh, what do you care?"

He gazed intently at her for a moment then sighed. "You're right. What do I care?"

"I don't know what Rachel sees in you." She practically spat out the words.

"Rachel likes me?" A silly grin spread across his face.

"I can't see why," she replied angrily and headed toward the back wall. She scooped up a bottle of sleeping medication, walked past Damian, and slammed the bottle on the counter. He was still rooted in the middle of the aisle when she left the store.

With every step home, her anger found its way to her feet. *Thump, thump, thump.* She didn't even care if she disturbed her neighbors as she stalked down the hall toward her apartment door.

Once inside her place, she realized her soles hurt as much as her heart. She swallowed two pills and chased them with a gulp of water. She wanted to block out everything that had just happened but couldn't.

Damian's words rang in her ears. Her only defense—how could she possibly stick by Nathan when he didn't want her to?

❧

Blessed sleep finally encompassed Stephanie, and she awoke feeling groggy and confused. It took several minutes to orient herself. Had she only slept a few hours again? In the distance, she could hear bells ringing.

Church bells. She sat frozen for a moment. Was it Sunday? *I did get some sleep after all. Thank You, God!*

She listened to the chimes peal and suddenly bolted upright. *Church! That's it. I've got to go to church.* How many years had it been?

Instantly, she sprang to life. After a rushed shower, she dressed quickly. She dug through an old chest until she found her mother's worn and faded Bible. Grabbing her keys, she headed for the only church she knew of nearby. She'd driven past it numerous times and hoped she wasn't too late.

When she pulled into the parking lot, families were still arriving. She went inside, found an empty pew, and slipped into it.

Someone sat at a large white grand piano, playing with passion. People greeted one another while children played and laughed. Her heart clenched. She thought coming here would be a wonderful experience. Instead, the ache within her ballooned.

Before she could escape, a young couple greeted her and sat down, blocking her in.

After the opening worship music stopped, the minister approached the pulpit. He told them he disliked giving announcements and decided to dispense with them—since they were all in the bulletin anyway—and do something different this morning.

"Many members of our church are suffering and in need of prayer. So often we squeeze praying for one another in at the end of the service. Usually, parents are rushing off to gather their children and people are distracted. So before we even hear the message this morning, I'd like to pray for those who need a touch from God.

"If we never get to the sermon, that's fine. We're here to do God's work, and I believe He wants to minister to His people this morning.

"I'd like to call a faithful member of our church forward. He has decided to leave our town, and I know we are going to miss him. He's been such a blessing to me, to all of us, and as a church I'd like to return that favor by praying for him and showing him we care. Nathan Moses, will you join me up here?"

Stephanie's heart stopped. She held her breath. She turned and watched him walk forward from the back of the sanctuary. He looked worn and tired. Even from this distance she could still see the bruise by his temple. His arm rested in a sling.

The pastor called for the elders of the church to come forward. When everyone lowered their heads to pray, she did, too, closing her eyes tightly and praying fervently. Nathan had lost his business and now his church. She felt awful.

When the service ended, she managed to maneuver out of the building and to her car before anyone spoke to her. She blinked hard and fast to keep the tears at bay.

Throughout the service, she believed God wanted her to help Nathan. Though she didn't know how or when, she understood now that she couldn't let him leave town without first clearing his name. Even if she had a responsibility to Heather. *There must be some way to solve both problems, Lord. Please help me find it.*

twelve

"Were you going to call and tell me you were leaving? Or were you going to slink out of town?" Stephanie demanded to know as she barged into Nathan's classroom. She'd been driving around for quite some time since slipping away from the church, and she ended up in his parking lot.

"Steph, you can't risk losing your job because you associate with me," he replied as he pulled a poster off the dingy wall.

"So why don't you tell me what really happened?"

"Heather told you what happened." He kept his back to her as he spoke.

"Do you want to know what she said?"

"I can imagine."

"Is it true?" She sat down at one of the desks, feeling overwhelmed and struggling with the despair that sought to smother her.

"To her, it probably was. Maybe I did neglect her a little. She seemed okay with everything, though she didn't join in much. I can understand her anger."

"Nathan, we both know the charges are false."

He dropped the box he had just picked up and turned to look at Stephanie. Color had drained from his face. "Did Heather tell you that?"

Stephanie shook her head. "I love you, or have you forgotten that?"

"You did what you had to do. Your first priority is to protect the kids."

A stab of disappointment sliced through her. He'd ignored her comment about still loving him. She wanted to throw something. "And what about you? You're going to run out? What about shaking off the dirt and moving up?"

"That's only a story," he said resignedly. "In cases like this

150

a man is guilty even if proven innocent, and then he's forever treated as a pariah."

"So you're leaving."

"God must have something better."

"You know, you really aren't like Moses at all." She waited a beat then went on. "Sure, he was a reluctant leader and hero like you, but in the end he still did the job he had been called to do. He didn't run out on the children of Israel."

"Stephanie, you've somehow put me up on some great pedestal. There's no place for me to go but down. I'm no hero—"

"You were to me," she said, fighting back tears. "You were to me." She got up and walked out praying he would follow her, but he didn't.

In that instant, she realized she didn't deserve happiness. Life wasn't some magical fairytale. Besides, who wanted to marry someone larger than life anyway?

She did.

❧

Stephanie knew Nathan would never have done what Heather said, but she had to report the incident. She had no choice. Dwelling on this, she drove to her office in a fog. Pulling into her designated spot, she turned off the car and rested her head on the steering wheel.

Moments later, a light tap on the car window startled her. When she turned, she saw Heather and wound down the window. "What are you doing here?"

"I need to talk to you," the girl said timidly.

"Let's go inside, shall we?"

Heather paced the office while Stephanie turned on some lights. "Have a seat, if you'd like."

"Thanks," she replied, but remained standing.

Once seated behind her desk, Stephanie pulled out a notepad and tape recorder. "Mind if I record our meeting?"

Heather nodded her assent. "What did you say to my folks when you dropped me off?"

"Why?"

"They're really mad at me. But I didn't do anything. Mr. Moses did."

"I only told them what you said."

"How come he's not in jail?"

"He's been released for now."

"Did he deny it?"

"No, Heather, he didn't."

"What did he say?"

"Does it matter?"

"Yes. I mean, no." Heather glanced around the room, never meeting Stephanie's gaze.

"When I found him with Damian, I asked what happened. He said he trusted you to tell the truth."

"And?"

"And that's all he would say."

Heather sank into the sofa. Stephanie could tell she was struggling and waited a few more minutes before speaking. "Is there something you want to tell me?"

"What will happen now?"

"For now, Nathan has closed down Burning Bush Adventures, and he can't be around female teenagers."

"Will he go to jail?"

"Probably. Of course, losing his company and the respect of everyone from the trip is probably worse than jail time for Nathan. You know how he is. He really cares about his job and the people he helps."

Heather stood. "He cared about everyone on that stupid trip but me."

Stephanie nodded for Heather to continue.

"He hugged Liz and Paula, even you. He joked with Keith, treated Ian like a buddy, and helped Tom. But me he simply ignored."

"Did he really?"

The girl began to pace in front of Steph's desk. "He never even thanked me for saving his life."

"I think you're wrong. I remember him saying how proud he was of you for not panicking. Didn't he mention how bad he felt about your blisters?"

"He walked with everyone and liked their company and treated me like an outsider."

"Sometimes we send out vibes that other people pick up on. Until recently, I held everyone at arm's length. I didn't even realize I was doing it. I was on the outside looking in. Even before the camp started, I felt like that."

"You did? But you're a counselor."

Steph smiled. "I did. And let me tell you, it's very lonely."

"So why'd you do it?"

"I didn't know I did until Nathan pointed it out."

"See, he even helped you."

"I think you're being too hard on him. And he's helping you a great deal."

"Sure," Heather said with a sneer.

Steph put down her pen. "I suspect he's protecting you, too."

"Huh? You've got to be kidding."

"Am I?"

"I knew you'd be on his side," she spat out, folding her arms in defiance.

"Tell me what really happened."

"I already told you."

"Okay, I'm going to tell you what I think happened." Steph came around to the front of her desk and leaned against it. "You were feeling neglected by Nathan. And because of that you maybe tried to get his attention. When he resisted you, you got angry. By the time you got back to us, you had torn your clothes to make it look like he assaulted you. Am I close?"

"Not even," Heather smirked. "Look at these." She pulled off her jacket and showed Stephanie the bruises on her forearms. "This is where he grabbed me and wouldn't let me go."

"Nathan is a very strong guy. How did you break free?"

"I hit him in the head."

"I don't think that would stop him."

"I guess I must've hit him where he'd been hurt because he fell to the—" She stopped mid-sentence.

"Go ahead, finish."

"He fell to the ground."

Suddenly things were falling into place. Nathan didn't follow Heather back to the camp because she must have knocked him out when she slugged him. Why else would he have fallen? *I'm sorry I didn't stick by you, Nathan.*

"And then you ran back to the camp?"

"Yes."

"Why didn't he follow you and finish what he started?"

"I—I don't know."

Stephanie pushed a bit more. "Nathan must care for you an awful lot."

"I told you, he ignored me the whole trip."

"And that bothered you, didn't it?"

"Yes. No!"

"Then why did it bother you when he started paying attention to you?"

"Because."

"What is he protecting you from?"

"He's not. He tried to kiss me." Heather's voice grew louder and the pitch higher.

"You're certain?" Stephanie asked in a calm voice.

"I am."

"I guess all his talk about things not being as they appear, dealing with adversity, and taking responsibility for our actions was merely a bunch of mumbo jumbo then. He probably did more damage than good where everyone is concerned. Well, he won't be able to do this to anyone again."

"Exactly." Heather nodded in satisfaction at Steph's words as she paced near the couch.

"Well, I guess that's it. Anything else you'd like to add?"

Heather shook her head.

"Oh, one more thing. Is this what you told Officer Luther?"

"I haven't spoken to anyone." Heather lowered herself back down onto the sofa. "Do I have to tell it all again in front of strangers?"

"You'll do fine. Testifying in court isn't much harder. I'll be there for you."

"In court?"

"Yes. First you'll tell Officer Luther. A court date will be set, and then you'll have to tell it again."

Heather gulped.

"This is very important, Heather. The more I listened to you talk, the more I realized that Nathan needs to be stopped. He can't go on like this, emotionally damaging kids and assaulting them. I opposed this right from the very beginning. I'll see to it that he never hurts another person."

"But he helped everyone else." Heather's tough facade seemed to be about to crack.

"Yes, that's right, you did say that."

Heather remained silent and fidgeted. The tension thickened until she finally sighed and tears began to flow. "What have I done?"

Stephanie moved to the sofa and embraced her. "Nothing that can't be fixed."

"He never touched me, Miss Harris," she said, sobbing into Stephanie's shoulder.

✵

"Damian, what an unexpected surprise. How did you know where I lived?" Rachel greeted him pleasantly.

Good, it would appear that Stephanie hasn't spoken to her yet about our encounter at the store. "Mind if I come in?"

"Sure," she replied as she opened the door wider. "I've been so worried about Steph. What happened out there?"

"This had to be the worse trip I've ever been on," he said as she led him into the sitting area.

"Steph hasn't returned my calls since she got back. I had no idea they came home early until I bumped into her boss. He is beside himself with worry for her. If I didn't know better, I'd say he cares for her."

"So she hasn't said a word to you?"

"Nothing. Can I get you something to drink? Coffee?"

"That would be nice. With milk and sugar, please." He watched as she got up and went into the small, tidy kitchen. Looking around, he admired the surroundings.

Rachel's apartment had much more character than Stephanie's. Numerous small paintings were displayed in unusual patterns on the walls, and the ornate frames matched the beveled and etched mirror over the gas fireplace. He felt comfortable here.

Rachel brought in a tray and set it down in front of him. On a plate were some sweet-smelling cinnamon rolls and chocolate chip cookies, as well as two cups of steaming coffee. She picked up one of the cups and handed it to him.

Gee, I could get used to this. "Thanks."

"I hope I didn't put in too much sugar," she said as she sat down.

He took a cautious sip. "Perfect."

"Okay, so tell me everything."

"What a disaster," he began as he told the long tale.

"I can see why Steph came home so upset." Rachel's face registered shock when he finished but not a trace of the contempt he'd expected.

"Steph knew all along that the desert was no place for those kids," he said.

"I thought she was uptight about this camp for no reason. I mean, after all, it had worked well in many other places."

"I think if it hadn't been run by Nathan but rather someone more qualified, it might have worked out better."

"Funny how first impressions can be so wrong. He seemed perfect for the camp and for Stephanie. I've been keeping my fingers crossed that something would develop between them. Steph deserves a nice guy. She's suffered so much—"

Damian watched as she bit her lip and stopped short. He began to feel guilty. He hadn't been much of a help on the trip. But he had his own problems to think about.

". . .family is really important."

"What? Oh, yes. I agree." *How did we start talking about family?*

"I think it would have helped Stephanie so much. You know she lost everyone in that accident."

"I didn't know."

"She's carried a burden of guilt about it all this time. I'd been hoping she would find in Nathan a soul mate. Then she could start her own family and get on with her life."

"I don't see that happening now."

"It's too bad, because if you have family, you have everything. Or at least that's what my dad says. Sometimes I'd like to trade them in, but when things have been tough, they've stood by me. I wouldn't trade that."

Damian wanted Rachel to stop talking. He needed to think. All of a sudden, everything he'd plotted didn't seem as important anymore. In fact, if things went as he had planned, he would probably never see his parents or siblings again. While a part of him felt they deserved what they got, the other side begged him to stop. Now. Before it was too late. He wondered how the total acceptance of one person—namely Rachel—could make this much difference in his life?

"Is something wrong, Damian?"

He shook his head. "No."

"The trip must have been a bit of a strain on you, too."

"More than you'll ever know." He put his coffee cup down and rose. "I've got to be going, Rachel. Thanks for everything."

She jumped up and followed him to the door. "Thanks for dropping by. Oh, by the way, you didn't tell me how you knew where I lived?"

"I can't tell you right now," he said as thoughts began to form in his mind. "But if you'll have dinner with me tomorrow night, I'll tell you all the details." *And I promise it will be more than you want to hear.*

"I'd love to."

"Good. See you around seven-thirty."

After Rachel closed the door, he looked at his watch. If he hurried, maybe he'd have enough time to catch his father before he left town for a business trip. If he told him the truth, would he ever see him again? Maybe. But if he went ahead with his original plan, he'd be disowned, orphaned like Nathan. He shuddered at the thought.

ïa

Stephanie fussed with the files on her desk as she talked with Phil. "Heather isn't going to press charges, and I'll make sure everything is clear in my incident report."

"You've been through a lot," he said with compassion.

"It wasn't so bad. And I've had a lot of time to reassess my own life."

"I hope you're not leading up to something I don't want to hear. In fact, before you say any more, I'd like to say something." He walked over to the large window in her office and closed the blind.

Was he going to fire her? "Sure, Phil. What's on your mind?"

"I know I'm a little bit older than you. In fact, I've always felt that you saw me as the father you never had, and I've been content with that—until you came back from this camp." He paced her office much like Heather had done the day before.

"I've been so worried about you. I even drove by your place each night but didn't have the courage to ring the buzzer."

Waves of shock coursed through her. She started to speak, but Phil held up his hand. "Let me get this out. Please."

She nodded.

"Like I said, I had no idea how much I cared, but now that I do, I wanted to know if you thought there'd be a chance for us."

"Us?"

"Steph, do you think you could ever love me? Well, what I mean is, I love you and I want to spend my life with you. I know you've been unhappy, but I would try my best to make you content. We get along well. Maybe you wouldn't love me as much as I love you, but sometimes those are the best marriages. We wouldn't be following our hearts blindly. . ."

His words rushed on like the river she'd seen in the desert. She felt as if she were drowning in a whirlpool.

How *did* she feel about Phil? Of course, it didn't matter because she loved Nathan. But Nathan wasn't staying. Phil would always be here. He was constant. He loved her and wanted to make her happy. Phil wasn't a hero to her, but he was a nice man. A tender man who'd take good care of her. Phil was the safe choice. But that wasn't what she wanted. In fact, his offer made it all so clear to her.

"You don't have to answer right now," he continued. "I'll give you some time if you'd like." He moved to her side and took her hands in his.

"I'm in a state of shock, Phil. But I promise you I will give your proposal serious consideration." She couldn't bear to hurt him. After all, she did love him. Just not that way.

"Take all the time you want," he whispered as he leaned down and placed a tender kiss on her forehead.

Stephanie closed her eyes when he kissed her. When she opened them, Phil had left her office.

&

It's been a pleasant dinner so far, but how will she react? Damian shifted uncomfortably in his chair. "Rachel, I need to tell you something that I hope won't change your opinion of me."

He watched her eyes open wide with wonder. "Okay," she said calmly.

"All my life, I've been like the runt in the family with my older brother being my father's pride and joy, and my younger sister owning his heart. I've never felt like I belonged." He moved his fork away from his plate then picked up his water goblet and put it back down. "I've been trying for years to make them take notice of me. I thought I'd found a way, too." He paused.

"Go on," she urged.

"They would take notice all right, because they would be wiped out financially. My father has sunk everything he owns into the new complex out by the highway. I found out which anchor retailers were in negotiations and convinced them to lease with me instead."

"I don't understand."

Damian wrung his hands beneath the table. "You will. Let me finish."

She smiled at him and nodded.

"I managed to buy some prime property. Actually, I convinced an elderly woman to sell it for half its value. I'm not proud of that. Even worse, I managed to convince Nathan to sell me his business and property for less than fair market value, too. Those two parcels of land, along with the two I already own, make for the perfect site for the largest shopping mall in Utah. Can you believe it, I got eight anchors?"

"What are anchors?" Rachel wiped her mouth with her napkin.

"Large retailers. They draw the customers. Stores like J.C. Penney, Sears, and Bon Marche. And we'll have a major cinema with IMAX theatres. Not only will it put us on the map, it will solidify my place in the business world." He paused. "And ruin the rest of my family."

Rachel stared at him blankly. "You can't be serious."

"I'm not proud of what I've done."

"It's not too late to back out, is it?" She leaned forward and touched his hand.

"I tried to see my father last night to tell him, but he'd left on a business trip."

"So you don't want to go through with it?"

"I've ruined so many lives so far, what difference would it make?"

"It takes a courageous man to admit his faults and make restitution. I don't think you're a coward, Damian."

"I can't make everything better. Nathan has probably left town—"

"Then track him down. You found my address and Steph's. You've obviously got resources."

"You don't hate me?"

"I don't think I could ever hate anyone. I'm disappointed, but I believe you'll do the right thing."

"Thanks for the vote of confidence." He sat back, his mind figuring quickly.

What should he do? Maybe he and his father could join

forces and work together. No, his father would never consider that. Could he possibly rectify everything by warning his father that the retailers were no longer backing him? No matter which option he chose, he'd look like a failure.

Did that matter now? He looked over at Rachel. She gazed at him with compassion in her eyes. How could the acceptance of this one woman make him want to be a better person? It was all so foreign to him, but he liked it.

æ

Stephanie drove faster than she preferred, praying she would not be too late. Rachel's bombshell had sent her into action. Damian may have confessed and had a change of heart, but it didn't change the mess he'd made of things.

How could Rachel still care for that guy?

It didn't really matter. What mattered was that Nathan could keep his camp. Damian would fix everything, and then she and Nathan could be together.

You haven't told him everything, that little nagging voice pierced her thoughts, sending a chill through her body.

There were no lights on in the classroom when she pulled up to the trailer and parked by Nathan's jeep. Maybe he was out in the Burr. She looked at her watch. He was probably home in bed by now.

What should I do?

Before she could finish asking the question, a light came on. She got out and walked up the steps. With her hand in midair to knock, the door suddenly flew open. She jumped back in surprise.

"Stephanie!" Nathan said. The yearning in his voice was obvious.

How she ached to fling herself into his arms, but she stood her ground. "Can I talk to you?"

He pulled the door back, and she stepped into the now bare-walled room. She sat down at one of the desks and took in a deep breath. Nathan stayed by the door watching her.

They both started to speak at the same time.

"You first," he offered.

"Rachel came to see me this evening. She'd had dinner with Damian."

Nathan grunted, then moved to a chair. "Bet he was gloating about the great deal he got for this place."

"Actually, he wasn't."

"That's a surprise. I wish I'd never met the guy."

"I'm not so sure you should feel that way. I think Damian taught us both a valuable lesson."

"Like I could learn anything from that complainer."

"Nathan, is it true you needed the state contract to keep your business going?"

He blinked. "How did you find that out?"

"Damian told me shortly after we first met."

"I knew I didn't like him," he snarled, folding his arms across his broad chest.

"I think you forgot to listen to your first rule."

"Don't anticipate problems? What's that got to do with this?"

"Okay, maybe it's not your first rule. But it's an important one. Trust—"

"You want me to trust Damian?"

"Would you let me finish please? You forgot to trust God. And believe it or not, you trusted Damian or me to keep your business going."

"You have a point there, but if you think I'm going to trust Damian or maybe even work for him, you can think again."

"Damian's not going to hold you to your agreement of sale."

"I don't want the business. I'm a man of my word, Steph. I agreed to sell it and I'm bound by that."

"But Damian wasn't honest with you. He took advantage of you. He slandered your business so you needed him. His actions were sneaky and underhanded."

"Doesn't matter. I agreed. That's it."

"You agreed based on a lie. You thought it was an honest deal, but it wasn't."

"That's merely a technicality."

Stephanie sighed in exasperation. "You also gave me your word out there that you loved me and wanted to spend the rest of your life with me, yet you're leaving town." She waved her hand over the packed boxes.

"Things changed."

"Another technicality?"

"I don't have any way to support a wife, I may have ruined your career, and I don't even have a place to hang my hat."

"So you'll get your business back, my career is fine—if I want it—and I know the perfect place to hang your hat." She jumped up from the desk, grabbed his hat from the coat rack, and placed it on her head.

He laughed. "You're right. I didn't trust God and I failed, Stephanie."

"Don't you see? You didn't fail. You were swindled by Damian, but everything is going to be okay." She could feel herself grasping at straws. No matter what she said, it looked like she would never convince him.

"All because I didn't trust God. I'm trusting Him now."

"So you're still going to run out?"

"I'm not running, Steph."

"You have to forgive yourself. Learn from this and move on. Isn't that what you'd tell the kids if they were here?"

"I should never have taken them out there."

"Nathaniel Moses, I could slap you. You changed my life for the better. I love you and want to be with you, and you're willing to throw me away."

"I have nothing to offer."

"Not even love?" she whispered, praying he wouldn't turn her away. It would be like losing her whole world again if he did.

He turned his back on her.

"You're lying to yourself, Nathan. I know you love me. But, here, let me give you a reason to hate me. That'll make it easier for you to leave me."

"What do you mean?" he asked as he turned around.

"Know why I wasn't on that hike with my family?" She choked back a sob. "Because my friend and I had been out shopping the day before, and she had stolen some perfume and put it in my pocket. I didn't know it, but they stopped us and searched me—and found it."

She moved away from Nathan as she continued. "I tried to explain to my folks, but this friend had gotten me into so much trouble prior to this that they didn't believe me. They grounded me, and I wasn't allowed to go with them. I was so angry. As they left, I shouted, 'I hope you never come back!' I truly never wanted to see them again, and I prayed they would all die."

Though it felt good to finally admit the truth to someone, facing it out loud ripped her apart. The tears flowed freely. In an instant Nathan moved to her side and reached for her hand.

"God knows you didn't mean that, Steph. He knows how much you loved them. You were hurt and lashing out. Think how young you were. We all say things we regret. At any age."

Steph sobbed. "God has been punishing me ever since. Until the day I met you. Then it seemed like His anger had finally stopped."

"Oh, my sweet, God was never angry with you. He would never punish you like that."

She withdrew from his touch. "He's still punishing me, because now you're leaving."

Nathan remained silent while Stephanie's sobs echoed in the room.

"My heart goes out to you, Steph. I've never loved you more than at this moment. All this pain you've carried by yourself. If it were in my power, I'd change the past. But I can no more change that than stay here. Don't you see? I love you enough to leave. You'd lose your job if I stayed. I'll never be free of the stigma attached to someone accused of assault."

"But the charges were dropped."

"Kids talk. Everyone knows what happened out there. I won't risk your reputation."

"Keith came to me that night and said he knew Heather wasn't telling the truth." She stopped begging when he stepped away, shaking his head.

"It's done, Steph."

"Where's your faith, Nathan? Do you think God would bring me into your life only to cast me away again? There must be some way we can resolve this. Damian doesn't want your business. He said that to Rachel."

"If he doesn't want it, what's going on?"

"I made an error in judgment," Damian said as he stepped through the door.

Stephanie and Nathan turned around in surprise.

Damian continued before they could speak. "I thought I needed it, but I don't." He tore up the contract as he spoke. "Nathan, I wasn't honest with you. I'm sorry. You know, I learned a lot from you out in that camp. And, surprisingly, I even found out a thing or two about myself." He paused and looked at the two of them. "Am I interrupting something?"

"No," Nathan replied.

"Well, anyway, the business is still yours. I owe you that much. I'd like to meet with you tomorrow to discuss a much better offer, if you're interested."

Nathan nodded.

"You know something else I learned?" Damian said. "There's nothing like family." He glanced at Stephanie and then back to Nathan. "Finding someone you care for is difficult, and a wise man would never let anything stand in the way of such love. He might never find anything like it again." He winked at Steph and left almost as quietly as he had entered.

"Who would ever have thought Damian could come to such a conclusion?" Stephanie asked.

Nathan laughed heartily. "Miracles do happen."

An uneasy silence fell upon them. Then they both started to speak again.

"You first," Stephanie said this time.

"I'm a pigheaded fool, aren't I?"

"Close, but not quite."

"You're too kind." He moved to embrace her tenderly.

"Does this mean—"

"Yep, whether you like it or not, I'm going to marry you."

"Oh, I like it real fine," she said, before his mouth covered hers with the passion of a man in love.

epilogue

"In the desert?"

"That's what I said." Stephanie laughed softly. "The look on your face is priceless!"

"You want to get married in the desert?"

"Until I met you, my whole life had been a dry, barren wasteland. You saw beauty in me, like in that arid locale you love so much."

Sitting in the huge tent, waiting nervously, she remembered that conversation as if it had been only last night. Hard to believe the words had been spoken a year ago. Today she would become Mrs. Moses. She could hardly wait for the moment when she would say "I do" and Nathan would kiss her for the first time as her husband. She had waited a lifetime for this moment.

The year had flown by and a lot had happened. The same group, including Damian and Rachel, had traveled back to the desert and completed the trip successfully. Damian's father agreed to join with his son and help develop the two pieces of land that Nathan and the elderly woman sold to him. Though things weren't resolved yet, they were working toward getting to know one another. Not an easy road for Damian, but Steph admired him for trying.

Recently, Rachel and Damian had become something of an item. Both of them now attended church with Nathan and her. Yes, it had been a very eventful year. Could things get any better?

Maybe Rachel will catch my bouquet!

All the kids were at the wedding, too. Heather would be singing, with Tom playing the portable keyboard. Keith and Ian were ushers. Liz and Paula had decorated the chairs and the makeshift sanctuary with lilac ribbon and matching flowers.

Phil had agreed to walk her down the aisle. It had been difficult for Stephanie to turn down his marriage proposal, but she knew she would only love him as a dear friend. At first disappointed, he now seemed genuinely happy for her.

"Where are you, Steph?" Rachel asked with a smile.

"Remembering this past year. God has been so good to me."

"To all of us." She handed Steph her lipstick.

"I can't even remember what my life was like before Nathan. He's filled every sad corner of my heart."

"And I'm sure you've done the same for him." Rachel giggled. "Do you remember how angry he made you when you two first met?"

"Don't remind me. I made such a fool of myself."

"Nathan didn't think so." They laughed again.

"Well, how do I look?"

Tears filled Rachel's eyes, and Steph felt her emotions rising to the surface as well. "Stephanie, you're so beautiful. I've never seen you so—so radiant. You're practically glowing."

"That's the perspiration from fear."

"Have we got everything? How does that go? 'Something old, something new, something borrowed, something blue'?"

"Something like that." Stephanie peered into the mirror while Rachel rearranged little strands of curls around her face.

For a long moment they simply stared at the crisp white gown. The sweetheart-neckline suited Stephanie. A heart-shaped locket hung from a simple gold chain. Inside were pictures of her mother and father.

Stephanie reached for the necklace and opened it.

"Maybe they're watching from heaven," Rachel said.

Steph hugged her best friend and then dabbed at the corners of her eyes.

Rachel laughed. "Don't you dare cry, Stephanie! We don't have time to reapply your makeup. Plus, you'll get me crying, too. Then Nathan will have to come in here and save us from all the water."

"Everyone ready in there?" Phil asked from outside the tent. "They've started the music."

Rachel pulled back the canvas flap and Phil entered.

"Wow! You look lovely, Stephanie. Nathan is a lucky man."

Stephanie took Phil's hand and squeezed it. "Thank you."

"It's time," Rachel said as she stepped outside the tent.

Phil and Steph waited a few minutes, and then he peered outside. "We're on." He took her arm and folded it over his elbow. "I wish you all the happiness in the world, Stephanie. And if you ever need me, you just call. I'll have lots of stories to tell your kids."

"I love you, Phil."

"Let's go meet your groom."

Stepping out of the tent, Stephanie experienced a rush of joy from all the faces smiling at her. She choked back tears of profound happiness with each step.

"Slow down," Phil whispered. "Nathan will wait for you."

She nodded in response to him and lessened her pace.

Raising her gaze to where the minister, best man, and groom stood, her eyes locked with Nathan's, and her heart did a quick two-step.

When she reached Nathan, he took her arm and Phil stepped back.

The minister began, "Dearly beloved, we are gathered here today to join this man and this woman. . ."

All too soon she heard, "You may now kiss your bride."

Nathan turned and cupped her face in his hands. His warm kiss sent butterflies dancing in the pit of her stomach. This was it. From now and forever, she would always be Mrs. Nathaniel Moses.

Rachel nudged Stephanie. "You can stop anytime now."

They pulled away from each other, and everyone shouted and clapped. A flushed Stephanie turned to face the guests, sorry that Nathan's kiss had ended. But she had the rest of her life to enjoy him.

"Ladies and gentlemen, may I present Mr. and Mrs. Nathaniel Moses," the minister said.

The clapping resumed as they walked the aisle back toward the tent. Guests tossed rose petals as they passed.

Alone inside their canvas room, Nathan kissed her again. "I love you, Mrs. Moses."

"And I, you."

"I'd like to take a walk out to the oasis after dinner."

"Really, why?"

"It's where I first fell in love with you."

She smiled, warmed by his comment. "So long as we don't ever go back to where the flash flood took place."

"Is that where you fell in love with me?"

"I like to think it's where I saved you," she teased.

"So you're the hero in the family, eh? Well, I think I can live with that."

"And I can live with you forever."

"Shall we spend the next forty years out here in the desert?"

"Now you really do sound like Moses. Don't you want to enter the Promised Land?"

He pulled her closer. "I already have."

A Letter To Our Readers

Dear Reader:

In order that we might better contribute to your reading enjoyment, we would appreciate your taking a few minutes to respond to the following questions. We welcome your comments and read each form and letter we receive. When completed, please return to the following:

Fiction Editor
Heartsong Presents
PO Box 719
Uhrichsville, Ohio 44683

1. Did you enjoy reading *Let My Heart Go* by Bev Huston?
   ❑ Very much! I would like to see more books by this author!
   ❑ Moderately. I would have enjoyed it more if

   _____

   _____

   _____

2. Are you a member of **Heartsong Presents**? ❑ Yes ❑ No
   If no, where did you purchase this book? _____

   _____

3. How would you rate, on a scale from 1 (poor) to 5 (superior), the cover design? _____

4. On a scale from 1 (poor) to 10 (superior), please rate the following elements.

   ____ Heroine   ____ Plot
   ____ Hero   ____ Inspirational theme
   ____ Setting   ____ Secondary characters

5. These characters were special because?_____

_____

_____

6. How has this book inspired your life?_____

_____

_____

7. What settings would you like to see covered in future
   Heartsong Presents books? _____

_____

_____

8. What are some inspirational themes you would like to see
   treated in future books? _____

_____

_____

9. Would you be interested in reading other **Heartsong
   Presents** titles? ❑ Yes ❑ No

10. Please check your age range:
    ❑ Under 18   ❑ 18-24
    ❑ 25-34   ❑ 35-45
    ❑ 46-55   ❑ Over 55

Name_____

Occupation _____

Address _____

City_____ State_____ Zip_____

Chesapeake

4 stories in 1

*T*he Chesapeake region of the mid-nineteenth century holds days tested by sorrow and renewed by hope. Meet four couples about to be faced with their greatest challenges—can they also find their greatest joys?

Author Loree Lough has woven four faith-filled tales of romance that are sure to bring heartwarming satisfaction.

Contemporary, paperback, 464 pages, 5 ³/₁₆"x 8 "

Presents

Great Inspirational Romance at a Great Price!

Heartsong Presents books are inspirational romances in contemporary and historical settings, designed to give you an enjoyable, spirit-lifting reading experience. You can choose wonderfully written titles from some of today's best authors like Hannah Alexander, Andrea Boeshaar, Yvonne Lehman, Tracie Peterson, and many others.

When ordering quantities less than twelve, above titles are $2.97 each.
Not all titles may be available at time of order.

SEND TO: **Heartsong Presents** Reader's Service
             P.O. Box 721, Uhrichsville, Ohio 44683

Please send me the items checked above. I am enclosing $ _____
(please add $2.00 to cover postage per order. OH add 7% tax. NJ add 6%.). Send check or money order, no cash or C.O.D.s, please.

To place a credit card order, call 1-800-847-8270.

NAME _____

ADDRESS _____

CITY/STATE _____ ZIP _____

HEARTSONG ♥ PRESENTS

Love Stories Are Rated G!

That's for godly, gratifying, and of course, great! If you love a thrilling love story but don't appreciate the sordidness of some popular paperback romances, **Heartsong Presents** is for you. In fact, **Heartsong Presents** is the premiere inspirational romance book club featuring love stories where Christian faith is the primary ingredient in a marriage relationship.

Sign up today to receive your first set of four, never-before-published Christian romances. Send no money now; you will receive a bill with the first shipment. You may cancel at any time without obligation, and if you aren't completely satisfied with any selection, you may return the books for an immediate refund!

Imagine. . .four new romances every four weeks—two historical, two contemporary—with men and women like you who long to meet the one God has chosen as the love of their lives. . .all for the low price of $10.99 postpaid.

To join, simply complete the coupon below and mail to the address provided. **Heartsong Presents** romances are rated G for another reason: They'll arrive Godspeed!

YES! Sign me up for Hearts♥ng!

NEW MEMBERSHIPS WILL BE SHIPPED IMMEDIATELY!
Send no money now. We'll bill you only $10.99 postpaid with your first shipment of four books. Or for faster action, call toll free 1-800-847-8270.

NAME_____

ADDRESS_____

CITY_____STATE_____ZIP_____

MAIL TO: HEARTSONG PRESENTS, P.O. Box 721, Uhrichsville, Ohio 44683
or visit www.heartsongpresents.com